MILTON MELTZER

CASE CLOSED

The Real Scoop on Detective Work

ORCHARD BOOKS / NEW YORK

An Imprint of Scholastic Inc.

For Ellen, Diana, Leonora, Julianne, Bronwen,
Maura, and Millie—my favorite snoops

—M.M.

Copyright © 2001 by Milton Meltzer

Page 86 represents an extension of the copyright page.

Library of Congress Cataloging-in-Publication Data
Meltzer, Milton, date.
Case closed: the real scoop on detective work / by Milton Meltzer.—lst ed.
    p.   cm.
Includes bibliographical references and index.
ISBN 0-439-29315-4
1. Detectives—Juvenile literature. 2. Criminal investigation—Juvenile
literature. [1. Detectives. 2. Police. 3. Criminal investigation.] I. Title.
HV7922.M45   2001   363.25—dc21   2001-016293

10 9 8 7 6 5 4 3 2 1   01 02 03 04 05

Printed in U.S.A.   24   Book Fair

First edition, September 2001
Photo research by Martin A. Levick
Book design by Mina Greenstein
The text of this book is set in 12 point Meridien Roman.

Contents

Part Three

Detective Work—
Not on the Police Force 55

Introduction

Headlines about crimes pock the pages of newspapers every day and are often the feature stories on radio and television newscasts.

You wonder, who committed the crime? And why? Will the guilty one be caught?

It's the detective's job to gather and analyze the evidence that may lead to an arrest, trial, and conviction. You probably believe that detectives know all the angles and "always get their man." That's the media's version—the detective as a clever, imaginative guy, hunting down crafty criminals. He roams the streets fearlessly for days, weeks, or months, trying to break a single case. Finally he solves the crime by his incredible deductive powers.

What is the work of detectives really like? (And it is women's work as well as men's.) How do they operate? What is their training? What are the tools of their trade? How successful are they? Are they subject to corruption? What risks do they run? What are their rewards?

In this book you'll find out about different types of detectives—police detectives and private detectives, forensic scientists, and investigative reporters—and the work they do to catch criminals. The skills they use in their work are supported by the efforts of many scientists, such as doctors, epidemiologists, archaeologists, and anthropologists, whose painstaking work helps detectives to solve mysteries.

After reading about the work of detectives—how they operate and what they achieve—some of you may be interested in pursuing a career in one of these fields.

Some say that detective work is only systemized common sense that can be applied to any problem. Is that so? Let's see.

PART ONE

What It's Like to Be a Detective

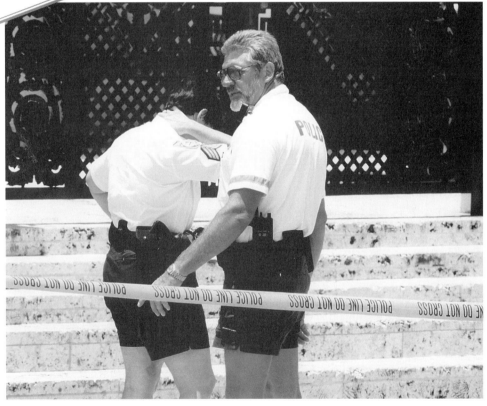

Miami police close off the bloodstained stairs of the mansion of Gianni Versace, the famous fashion designer, where he was mortally wounded upon his return home. Such stains may prove to be of great importance in the criminal investigation.

1
Uncovering Secrets

Detectives detect. "To detect" comes from the Latin verb "to take the roof off," which, in turn, can mean "to uncover what is hidden." The job of detectives, then, is to reveal the secret actions of criminals. They do it by investigating—by tracing or tracking evidence, and by using the power of systematic observation and clear thinking to discover the cause of a crime and arrest the criminal.

You'll find nothing about detectives in the records of early America. The colonists were suspicious of government officials who might spy on people and make trouble for them. For decades after independence they relied on watchmen, helped by civic-minded private groups, to keep down vice and crime. Respectable citizens formed vigilance committees whenever fear arose that vicious elements might threaten the community.

But as industry sprang up and cities grew large, more and more "bad eggs" were sniffed. Rapid growth of the population and the influx of great numbers of immigrants brought in lots of strangers. In the old, small communities, you knew who the good-for-nothings were—or thought you knew. But in the cities or in any new community, how could you spot the swindlers, the crooks, the violent ones?

Of course, professional criminals did not parade around with badges telling who and what they were. They dressed and talked like members of polite society. They could cheat you only if they concealed their criminal nature.

Out of necessity, then, the mid-nineteenth century created detectives. The first municipal detective squads were formed in Boston in 1846, New York in 1857, Philadelphia in 1859, and Chicago in 1861.

The notion of using specialists to catch criminals is fairly old. In Britain detec-

The British robber and thief-taker Jonathan Wild

tion was the responsibility of the injured person, his or her friends, or anyone else who wished to bother. True, there were justices of the peace, parish constables, and night watchmen. But they couldn't handle all the troublemakers. So the occupation of "thief-taker" sprang up. Drawn by the promise of rewards, private citizens, mercenaries, even criminals themselves hunted for lawbreakers. Constables naturally had connections with the underworld. Promised a good price, they would get back stolen property—unofficially, of course.

One of the most notorious thief-takers was Jonathan Wild (1683–1725), who melded the roles of detective and thief. He specialized in recovering stolen goods and proudly dubbed himself the "Thief-Taker General of Great Britain and Ireland." You applied to his "Lost Property Office" to get back what had been stolen from you, and prepared to pay a good price, naturally. Often the criminals Wild brought to justice were his competitors—rival gangs poaching on his territory. He became rich and famous, only to end up on the gallows.

Wild's methods were familiar in America. Constables in Boston and New York acted like thief-takers, making deals with criminals. Their victims paid gladly to get at least some of their goods back. The corruption spread, and by 1870 some New York detectives were found to be making deals with thieves. In return for not arresting the thief, the detective would be handed the plunder. He would then give two-thirds of the stolen goods back to the victims and split the other third with the thief. For this to work, the underworld had to know who these thief-takers were.

A New York detective of that era, George McWatters, described this in a book about his profession. He said that "the detective is dishonest, crafty, unscrupulous, when necessary to be so. He tells black lies when he cannot avoid it, and white lying, at least, is his chief stock in trade." But, he went on, the detective can ease his conscience by the knowledge that the trickery and falseness are all in the interests of justice. He is society's defense against the problem of secret, complex, mobile crime. Sometimes it takes lies and shams to counter lies and shams.

So the experienced detective becomes a master of pretense. He needs to develop the skills of an actor. He has to be able to disguise himself and to play many roles. A New York police chief, George Walling, said that just as the thief "ingratiates himself among honest men in order to plunder them, so the honest man associates with thieves in order to frustrate their plans." Said another detective, "I take pride in being able to read men at a glance, in being able to know a bogus story from a real one."

This playacting is only part of a detective's work. Much of what he does is less glamorous than scientific.

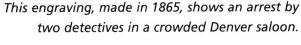

This engraving, made in 1865, shows an arrest by two detectives in a crowded Denver saloon.

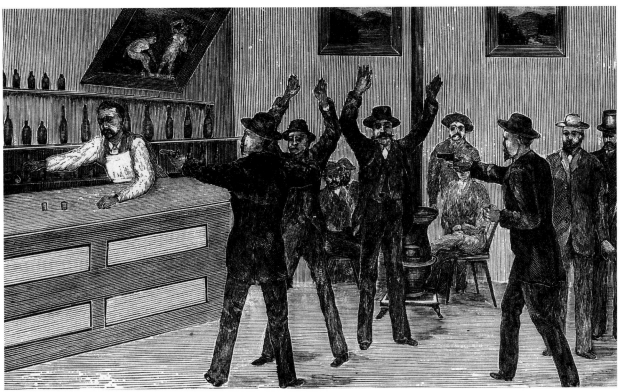

2 The Six Questions

Police headquarters receives a report that a crime has just been committed. Whatever its nature, detectives are rushed out to inspect the scene. They seek the answers to six questions: Who? What? When? Where? How? Why?

Until these are answered, the investigation isn't completed. The *who* has two parts: who is the victim? And who committed the crime? It's usually not hard to figure out the first who. But it is often much harder to find out who did it. All the knowledge and tools of police science are primarily focused on that one question: who committed the crime?

What was the crime? If an assault, what was done to the victim? If it is robbery, what was taken and what is its value? If arson or vandalism, what was destroyed? If a narcotics offense, what were the drugs? The answers may determine how the offense is classified and therefore the nature and degree of punishment.

When did the crime occur? The victim, if alive and conscious, usually can answer this. But if not, scientific analysis is needed to help find the answer.

Where did the crime occur? Right on the spot to which the detective is summoned? Or has the victim been moved? Again, close analysis is needed.

How was the crime committed? By what means? Anything special or peculiar about the circumstances?

And finally, *why* was the crime committed? If the reason is established, then it may suggest what kind of person to look for as a suspect.

3 Observation—Plus

If you have read any of the stories about the master fictional detective Sherlock Holmes, you get the impression that detectives can solve cases merely by looking at the hands or clothing of a suspect. In *The Hound of the Baskervilles*, for example, a man drops in on Holmes while he is out and leaves behind his cane. Holmes comes in later and deduces that his visitor was a country doctor, "under thirty, amiable, unambitious, absentminded, and the possessor of a favorite dog, which I should describe roughly as being larger than a terrier and smaller than a mastiff."

Observation! That was Holmes's first principle of detection. Sometimes as he scanned a crime scene he strengthened his sensitive eye with a magnifying glass.

Or take Allan Pinkerton, no fictional detective but a real one. He believed that professional criminals capable of daring crimes almost always left some clue by which their character as criminals could be established and subsequently their identity pretty clearly arrived at. He boasted:

An illustrator's portrayal of Sherlock Holmes and Doctor Watson, his associate, spotting the suspect in The Hound of the Baskervilles *as his carriage rolls by.*

In my thirty years of detective work these things became so marked and fixed that, on reading a telegraphic newspaper report of a large or small robbery, with the aid of my vast records and great personal experience and familiarity with these matters, I can at once tell the character of the work, and then, knowing the names, history, habits and quite frequently the rendezvous of the men doing that class of work, am able to determine, with almost unerring certainty, not only the very parties who committed the robberies, but what disposition they are likely to make of the plunders, and at what points they may be in hiding.

Holmes and Pinkerton used the most up-to-date detection tools available to them. Today, however, modern detectives are blessed with tools scientists hand them almost daily. You may have heard of lasers, ultraviolet light, spectrographs, neutron-activation analysis, DNA, computer software, scanning electron microscopes, blood grouping. . . . All these and more help to identify what can't be seen, and to analyze what can be seen.

Still, all the most sophisticated technology is sometimes so much junk unless something called serendipity comes into play.

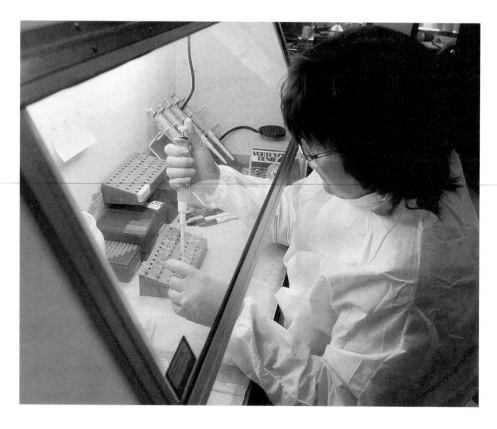

A researcher in the Colorado Bureau of Investigation's forensic laboratory works on DNA evidence in a murder case.

4
A Mold on a Petri Dish

What is serendipity? It's the gift of finding valuable things you weren't looking for. You can see how it operates in the physical sciences, where many important discoveries are made by serendipity. The researcher comes across something new, perhaps some relationship that couldn't have been foreseen. Take the way Alexander Fleming discovered the antibiotic penicillin. A bacteriologist in a London hospital, Fleming was trying in 1928 to isolate a vicious germ responsible for boils. One day he noticed that on one of the petri dishes in which he was cultivating bacteria, the germs were not growing as they should. In fact, they were dying. A foreign substance had apparently blown in through an open window and settled on the dish. A clear ring in the center of the dish showed where the invader had wiped out the germs.

Fleming had not planned for this to happen. He had never heard of it happening. Still, he sensed that the battle taking place on his petri dish was very meaningful. He applied his research methods to find out what was taking place. The foreign substance on the dish proved to be a mold of the common penicillium family, found in the air, on the ground, in the moldy bread in garbage pails. Fleming managed to isolate a tiny quantity of the brownish secretion. It proved to be a germkiller of great power. He named it penicillin. The drug worked wonders in laboratory animals and, then, during World War II, on thousands of the wounded. As mass-production methods were developed by the pharmaceutical companies, penicillin began to save millions of lives worldwide. So a chance event, grasped by a receptive mind, triggered one of the most momentous and far-reaching of all scientific achievements: the ability to harness microscopic living creatures in the service of humankind.

Like Sir Alexander Fleming, a detective must have an open mind, patience,

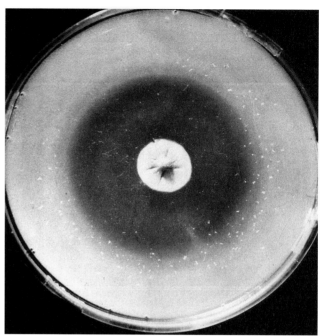

Sir Alexander Fleming

Penicillin in a petri dish

and perseverance. And as with scientists, it takes training over a long period of time to build all the specialized skills and knowledge a good detective needs.

When that penicillin mold sailed through Fleming's window and settled on his petri dish, the effect wasn't something he expected or something he was looking for. But, remember, he *noticed* it.

That power of observation is what makes detectives successful too. All their specialized training would be wasted if they were not skilled observers. Think about it for a moment and you can see why. When detectives arrive at the scene of the crime, they don't know what may turn out to be a vital clue. Could it be this scrap of cloth? These cigar ashes? This button? That Lincoln penny? The value of such odds and ends as clues may become clear only as the investigation proceeds. Overlook the critically important clue and the crime may go unsolved. That's why keen observation is so important when investigation of the crime scene begins.

A scientist may work on one problem all his professional life, but detectives face a vast variety of challenges. Every case presents something new—a mystery, a puzzle that tests their intelligence and experience. No wonder a detective's job is so fascinating.

5 On the Crime Scene

Let's follow how detectives in the homicide section operate. Notified of a dead body found at a street intersection and of two possible witnesses, they make careful notes of what they've been told and then move out to the scene. They find that the reporting patrolman has blocked off the area with yellow crime-scene tape. People are standing around, trying to get a closer look at the body.

The detectives don't have much to go on. They start by making a diagram of the crime scene, noting the position of the body on the ground, its location in relation to the surroundings, and the exact site of whatever objects are visible—a beer can, a cigarette butt, a glove, a stick.

Every time a crime occurs involving physical contact, the perpetrator leaves something at the scene, takes something away, or both. Soil, hair, fibers, powder, dust, a flake of skin, or any number of other things can become evidence of great value. This is called trace evidence and it's often easy to overlook, so the detectives practically vacuum the entire scene. Any samples they find are carefully logged and labeled, to be passed on to the forensic laboratory for analysis.

At the lab, a simple sight-reflected microscope can enlarge the samples by a factor of one thousand. If more power is needed, then the scanning electron microscope comes into play. It can compare such evidence as paint fragments, fibers, wood, and paper—even when they are as small as one hundred-thousandth of an inch. This instrument can also provide photomicrographs—photographs of microscope images—for use as evidence in court.

If it is hard to tell exactly what a sample is made of, then instruments using the principle of spectrography may provide the identification.

What microscopic trace evidence can do was demonstrated in a crime that horrified the country—the kidnapping in 1932 of Charles Lindbergh's infant son. Lindbergh was a hero, the first person to fly solo across the Atlantic. A ransom was paid, but the baby had been murdered shortly after he was kidnapped.

Two years later Richard Bruno Hauptmann, an immigrant carpenter, was arrested and tried for the crime. The critical evidence came from Arthur Koehler, a wood technologist. By the most painstaking work he traced the ladder used in the kidnapping back to the lumberyard from which its parts had come. He dissected the ladder into its several kinds of wood and probed them and the ladder's construction with microscopes, calipers, and a variety of lighting and photographic techniques. Gradually the ladder gave up its secrets. In Hauptmann's garage a variety of tools were found whose markings compared with those from the ladder.

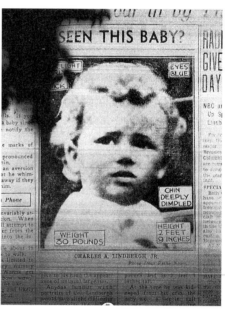

Above: This newspaper clipping showed the Lindbergh baby in the hope that someone would spot the missing child and notify the police.

Left: These sections of the ladder used by Richard Bruno Hauptmann became vital evidence in his trial.

To Link—or to Clear?

The scientists who analyze trace evidence make objective observations of the microscopic particles of substances or things left behind at the scene of a crime. Their observations are "objective" because their aim should not be to help a prosecutor convict. Trace analysis should seek to *link*—or to *clear*—a suspect. Laboratories that perform materials analysis ideally keep a sample collection of everything from car paints to domestic plastics. Any match ought to be confirmed by proven research using two different scientific methods. Written reports of both methods and findings should be kept on permanent file.

These bloodstained wood chips were evidence in the trial of a doctor who was accused of killing his wife. Tests of the blood failed to link the doctor to the crime.

Hauptmann was convicted and sentenced to death. Congress made kidnapping a federal offense, and in some states it is punishable by the death penalty.

What evidence of wood did to settle the Lindbergh case a single overcoat button did to convict William Dorr, who murdered millionaire George Marsh in 1912 in Massachusetts. A scrap of woven cloth with a pearl-gray overcoat button attached was found near the victim. Was it from the killer? Only by finding the overcoat could its significance be determined. The coat was found with all the buttons removed. But the piece of multicolored cloth on the button picked up at the crime site matched the coat in both weave and texture. The detectives speculated that as the victim fought for his life, he must have torn the overcoat button from the coat of the killer. Later the murderer had removed all the other buttons in the hope of preventing an identification. Soon after he did this, partly by chance, the detectives were led to the probable killer. Investigation showed he had a motive for the crime. But it was the single overcoat button that sent the murderer to the electric chair.

6 Scared Witnesses

When detectives have finished gathering evidence at the scene of a crime, what do they do next?

They look for witnesses. These aren't easy to find. People standing around when a crime occurs usually don't want to get involved. They're afraid. Thomas McKenna, a New York detective, tells what he does then:

> I have a step procedure I use in these cases. The first step is to get the witness to admit he heard the shot. If you can get him that far along, you have a live witness. Why? Because we know that any person on the street, or anywhere, who hears a shot, instinctively does two things: he ducks and he looks. Duck and look. To duck is the first instinct. The next is to make sure whoever is shooting is not shooting at you—so you look. Another instinct is to get away, get out of the way. The witness looks to see where the shooting is coming from, so as not to run right at the shooter while trying to get away from him.
>
> So you say to your witness, "Okay, you heard the shot, so you looked. You had to look. You wanted to get away from the shooter, whether he was shooting at you or not, so you had to look. You couldn't get away from the shooter if you didn't know where he was. You looked, pal. So tell us what you saw."
>
> The next thing you say is, "I suppose you didn't see the guy fire the shot. No. You looked after you heard the shot. What you saw was the guy standing there with the gun in his hand. You can't testify that you saw the guy shoot the gun, and I'm not asking you to testify to that. Hey, I'm your friend. I wouldn't ask you to testify you saw the guy shoot the gun when you didn't. All I want you to say is what you saw, that the guy had the gun in his hand."
>
> This is the way you work on a witness, step by step. It's not a quick process. Sometimes it takes hours.

Most witnesses are afraid even to talk to detectives. Those who will talk are often reluctant to sign a witness statement. They're scared to testify in court. Pete Razanskas, a veteran detective on the Los Angeles police department, said, "It's brutal these days to get people to testify. You go out on a crime scene and nobody sees nothin'. It's gotten bad. . . . I had a case where a guy gets shot in a bar. The place is packed that night, more than sixty people inside. Everyone I interviewed told me the same things: 'I was in the bathroom. I didn't see a thing.' I'm shaking my head after this. I turn to my partner and say, 'This is one bathroom I got to see. It's gotta be the biggest bathroom in LA.'"

Yet citizen cooperation in solving crimes is often crucial. Some detectives have a natural talent for getting information from people who don't normally confide in cops. Typically, a detective finds informants in bars, alleys, and other criminal hangouts. But in more elegant settings too. David Durk, who served many years on the New York City police force, said he found dinner parties often a rich hunting ground. Guests eating and drinking happily and finding themselves next to an off-duty detective would casually give away leads. One might talk about how bids were being rigged for construction of a new office building. Another might tell how to get goods through customs without paying duties. A woman might confide her internal conflict over what to do about her housekeeper's son, who is wanted for murder.

Investigation of a crime is a lot of hard work. Detectives will canvass a neighborhood, talk maybe to hundreds of witnesses or potential witnesses, seeking facts, facts, facts. Little things they say may add up to a big thing and lead to a successful prosecution.

A detective talks with a possible witness in a casual setting.

Informers are often important, says Thomas McKenna. "Obviously, we always keep their identities secret. . . . They can be all kinds of people. Some of them are paid. Some inform because of real or imagined favors done them by police officers. Occasionally we can put in a good word with the prosecutors on behalf of somebody else, a relative or friend of the informer.

"The fact is, most of them want to tell you something. The guy you're questioning hopes he can get away with telling you something that will make you believe he's not the bad guy. There is no end to the lines they will try to put over on you."

What witnesses have to tell a detective is sometimes shaped by the press. A reporter who has gotten to the witness first may not just ask what he or she saw but suggest what he wants the person to say, to back the story he wants to write. After being asked several times, "This is what you saw, isn't it?," a witness may well begin to believe that's what he *did* see.

A police officer talks with a boy living in a neighborhood where a crime has taken place.

Electronic Witnesses: Secret Listening, Secret Watching

In the 1990s videotape and audiotape began to dramatically alter American standards of evidence. Their use in several high-profile investigations established the truth of what happened.

The secretly audiotaped conversations between Linda Tripp and Monica Lewinsky played a big role in the House of Representatives' 1998–1999 case for the impeachment of President Bill Clinton on the charges of perjury and obstruction of justice. (The president was not convicted.)

When top executives of two giant American and Japanese food companies discussed business over a lunch in 1993, a video camera secretly hidden in a lamp recorded everything they said. The result was a huge price-fixing investigation that culminated in the charge of conspiracy to fix prices at the cost of the consumer.

Bugging devices are often used for political ends. Here, Gerry Adams, president of the Sinn Fein party of Northern Ireland, holds up a high-tech listening and digital tracking device found in a car.

When questioning a witness or a suspect, a most important skill is to be able to direct the conversation—not to let it reach a dead end, but to keep it going until the person tells you what you want to know. David Durk was said to use a psychological approach sensitive to the personality before him. He could appeal to a witness's idealism, to his natural desire to unburden himself, as well as to his fear. Durk knew when to press an issue and when to back off. He would let a conversation wander pointlessly at times, then circle back to a sensitive question from an unthreatening angle.

When talking to a witness, a detective may show him or her several "six-packs." These are sheets containing six photographs, one of which is of a suspect. Pete Razanskas always watches the witness's eyes when he or she looks at those photos. Even witnessses who lie to detectives, and say no one looks familiar, will always stare for a second or two at a photo of someone they recognize.

7 White-Collar Crime

Not all the people who do the work of detectives are on the police force. New York City has a Department of Investigation (DOI) with a multimillion-dollar budget and hundreds of people on staff. They are a kind of special police charged with fighting corruption. Their targets are people doing business with the city as well as city employees and officials engaged in illicit practices. Hundreds of such people caught at dirty work are arrested each year.

No detective work is easy or without risk. Nor is the work in the DOI. Pay is low, and the results of their work get little press attention. Yet their investigations nab people stealing public money and save the lives of citizens who could have been the victims of shoddy or criminally neglectful work.

Take those phony employment agencies that hired immigrants to do the dangerous work of removing asbestos from buildings. Undercover investigators found that the agencies were sending out workers on asbestos-removal jobs without the required protective equipment or without teaching them the skills needed to protect occupants of those buildings. Years later the removal workers and the building occupants could come down with a fatal lung disease. Arrest of the agency operators cost them five years in prison and a fine of $250,000 each.

The DOI concentrates mostly on white-collar crime. This huge category of offenses is often ignored or goes unpunished. Yet tax evasion, price fixing, embezzlement, consumer fraud, bribery, and swindling run through society, especially at its higher and wealthier levels. Such crimes cost the nation and the public hundreds of billions of dollars every year. That sum is more than ten times greater than the combined total from larcenies, robberies, burglaries, and auto thefts.

Violent crime, street crime, causes shock and pain and loss. All the worse because the victim is face-to-face with the criminal. But white-collar crime can be violent too, even though the harm it does is not face-to-face. When the untrained worker doing his job poorly, under a forged license, fails to remove asbestos properly and safely, he and the other victims will suffer the ruin of their health in years to come. But the prosperous owners of those corrupt agencies put profits ahead of the safety and lives of their employees and the public.

Even physicians can go bad. The DOI nailed one of them serving in the Bronx, New York. While maintaining his private practice, the doctor was also paid by the city to examine corpses of people who might have died of other than natural causes, then to visit family and neighbors to inquire about the dead person's condition before death. Finally, he was required to file a detailed report on his findings.

The doctor did his job well enough for years, then got tired of it. But instead of simply quitting, he wanted to go on pocketing the fees from the city's medical examiner's office. So he filled out the necessary forms without ever going to examine the corpse or to interview the neighbors and family. Meanwhile he continued with his thriving private practice.

Eventually, his fraudulence was discovered when he repeatedly failed to show up to examine the corpse or to interview the family, and complaints were lodged. Two detectives staked out his home while other cops watched for his presence at death scenes. When his fakery was amply proved, they had him.

Because such white-collar crime is often treated more leniently by the courts, and because the doctor was a dignified 67-year-old white man, he was sentenced only to a five-thousand-dollar fine and four hundred hours of community service. Chances are that some of those corpses he failed to examine had been murdered but were declared dead of natural causes. What happened to their killers?

Sadly, that Bronx doctor's trickery is hardly rare in his profession. Medical fraud of many kinds goes on all the time. A drugmaker was convicted of misrepresenting the safety and effectiveness of a drug used in treating premature infants. Government investigators found that thirty-eight infants had died of symptoms associated with the drug's use.

The biggest bank or payroll robberies committed by individual thieves or gangs have amounted to $5 or $6 million at most. But according to a Senate subcommittee investigation, white-collar crime—crimes committed by company executives, in large or small corporations—can run to over $200 billion annually.

In his book *Secret Police: Inside the New York City Department of Investigation*, Peter Benjaminson lists hundreds of cases investigated by that staff that resulted in arrests and convictions in the space of only a few years. Here are just a few examples:

- Twenty-seven building inspectors extorted over $150,000 from building owners, contractors, engineers, and architects in exchange for obtaining certificates of occupancy.
- Restaurant owners bribed undercover city inspectors not to cite them for violating health codes.
- Nine employees of the Department of Correction accepted bribes to smuggle cocaine to inmates in jails.
- Executive from a not-for-profit agency funded by the city made personal and illegal use of city agency funds.

Swindlers in Cyberspace

While violent crime has dropped nationwide in recent years, white-collar crime has skyrocketed. A booming economy, say law enforcement officials, breeds white-collar crime. Such crime rose 10 to 20 percent between 1995 and 2000, according to the National White Collar Crime Center.

Swindlers are making use of the Internet to cheat people out of their money and disappear into cyberspace. The FBI has 2,400 agents busy investigating some 26,000 white-collar cases, many involving the new technology. The increase in white-collar crime is felt most acutely in the financial centers of the big cities. Street criminals too are moving into the world of white-collar crime because it's easier to get away with it. A mugging can often produce a quick arrest. But there are so many ways to hide a white-collar job that it's much harder to convict in front of a jury.

Big money is made by white-collar criminals through investment fraud. Americans lose an estimated $40 billion a year to unscrupulous salespeople pitching everything from phony sweepstakes to phony stocks and bonds. The chief instrument for these swindlers is telemarketing. Of the 140,000 telemarketing operations, about 10 percent are engaged in fraud. More than half of the victims are over fifty. And a sizeable number of the swindlers are young, often teenaged. They have no conscience about swindling unsuspecting investors out of their savings, sometimes ruining their lives.

8
The Narcotics Squad

America has been fighting a war on drugs for decades. An epidemic of heroin use, especially among young blacks, spread with ferocious speed in the 1960s. Amid extreme racism, and an economy that seemed to have little use for them, these young people were a ready market for heroin traffickers. Many people saw drugs take over the lives of friends and relatives. Crimes that provided easy money shot up—shoplifting, purse snatching, burglary, theft of every sort, especially automobile break-ins. So did the more physically threatening crimes: muggings and holdups.

Yet no victory is in sight. Drug crimes are especially hard to deal with for many reasons. For one, the kinds of drugs used change often. For another, people who sell and people who buy willingly break the law. So they rarely want to call the cops. Patrol officers on their shifts have so many other problems to worry about that small-time street dealers are often left alone. It is the specialized narcotics officers who concentrate on big busts of wholesalers.

Drug abuse isn't a problem only of people at the lower levels of society. Today it cuts across all social and ethnic groups and classes. One estimate in 1998 held that 23 million people used illegal drugs. Of these, about half a million were heroin addicts and nearly 6 million were cocaine users. Huge numbers of users and dealers are now in prison for drug-related crimes. They account for about 60 percent of all federal prisoners and 20 percent of state prison inmates. Yet the most powerful and violent drug criminals tend to escape imprisonment.

The assignment of police to undercover narcotics work is a tough one, and one that can easily lead to corruption. The police may be bribed to look the other way or be paid off in drugs, or they may steal drugs from dealers and set up their own operation. Some police become addicts while making drug buys with taxpayers' money.

Fresh out of the police academy in Los Angeles, Michael Middleton was asked to become an undercover narcotics officer in Juvenile Narcotics. They chose him because although he was twenty-one, he looked about seventeen. The police suspected several boys were drug dealers in the high school where Middleton was sent. His job was to attend classes, do the work of any student, and make friends with the suspects. A tough task, because they'd had the same circle of friends for many years and might deal only within that group. A kid coming in from the outside would be viewed with suspicion.

Since narcotics use by undercover officers is forbidden, except in a life-or-death situation, Michael had to prove he was trustworthy without doing drugs with suspects. But he managed to make progress with one suspect by confiding that he was a burglar. That impressed the boy, who begged to go along with him next time he hit a place. Michael drove around with the boy to show him some houses he had supposedly robbed. The boy said he too had burglarized some stores and even robbed a guy one night at gunpoint.

Finally the undercover cop got one of the suspects to deliver some marijuana for him at an arranged drop-off point in an alleyway. That was followed by more buys and then an arrest of two students for selling narcotics.

Later Middleton was shifted to another high school, this time in the San Fernando Valley. Again undercover work brought about the arrest of a student drug dealer.

Middleton would spend twenty-one years on the Los Angeles police force, retiring as a sergeant to operate his own private investigation company.

A U.S. Customs agent in Seattle, Washington, discovers a huge shipment of cocaine stashed in the hold of a boat.

9
A Tough Job

Anyone who thinks detectives solve most crimes is sadly mistaken. This is not to say that they don't try their hardest. As we saw in chapter 2, their job is to gather facts and collect evidence that they hope will provide answers to the six key questions. But those answers are often not at all easy to come by. Nor do the conditions detectives work under make the job a dream.

A national study made by the U.S. Department of Justice in 1997 showed that many types of crime don't get much attention. Less than half of all reported crimes receive serious investigation, which might mean a month's work. Many times detectives have big backlogs of unsolved cases, cases that occurred in the past but which are still their responsibility.

In Kansas City, for instance, it was found that detectives generally worked on a case for a day, after which the case was either completed or suspended. The exceptions were cases of homicide, rape, burglary of safes, armed robbery, forgery, or counterfeiting. About 85 percent of this city's cases were suspended by the end of the first week.

In Miami, a big city in Dade County, Florida, homicide became so common around 1980 that the murder rate shot up to number one in the nation. Daily reports were so frequent that the newspapers would cram a dozen killings into one story. Most whodunits in Dade County remain unsolved.

Homicide detectives in quieter places can spend weeks or even months on a single murder, lining up witnesses, chasing every lead. Not so in south central Los Angeles, where detectives are so busy that "they do as much as they can, as fast as they can, until the next homicide," writes Miles Corwin of the *Los Angeles Times*. They "lurch from one dead body to another, from emergency to emergency." A typical weeknight in that neighborhood can see three murders in three hours, all within one square mile.

What may bring a tighter focus on a murder case is media attention. If reporters publicize a murder, police department bigwigs usually respond. They'll assign more staff on the job, put more pressure on them, and will follow the investigation more closely. High-profile crimes are the ones that consume more resources.

To crack old cases, New York's Police Department in 1996 set up a Cold Case Squad, a detective unit that follows up on unsolved cases that the regular detective squads lack the time or resources to deal with.

In its first three years, the unit cleared 280 old homicide cases, 180 of them by making arrests on cases they had built, 61 by capturing suspects who had evaded other detectives, and 39 by "exceptional clearance," usually meaning that the suspects had died.

The thirty-six detectives in the Cold Case Squad are veterans, with from fifteen to thirty years of experience each. Advances in technology, such as computer networks and better DNA testing methods, help the squad, but much of their success has been old-fashioned police work. That is, talking to people and getting them to talk. As one of them told a *New York Times* reporter, "It's my interaction with the witnesses. Sometimes people will tell you something important and they don't even know they're telling you. But you walk out of there knowing you just hit the gold mine."

Then, too, sometimes old cases are easier to solve because so much time has passed that people are less reluctant to speak to the police. One referring detective has pointed out that friends or family of a suspect may have had a falling-out with that person in intervening years, for example, so they may be more forthcoming and less likely to protect him or her.

Not only are detective squads overburdened; they often suffer the effects of steep cuts in city budgets. In Los Angeles, for instance, during the 1980s and 1990s cutting costs on essential equipment meant homicide detectives had to buy the beepers they were required to carry, their cellular phones, their camera kits, even the plastic nametags they wear at crime scenes. Nor did the department have a computer network to link its eighteen geographic divisions. So information such as crime patterns and trends couldn't be distributed swiftly throughout the city. Some detectives had to buy their own laptop computers and printers to write their reports and had to drive beat-up old squad cars.

When you're overworked, understaffed, and underequipped, a tough job is made all the tougher.

PART TWO

Behind the Scenes in the Lab

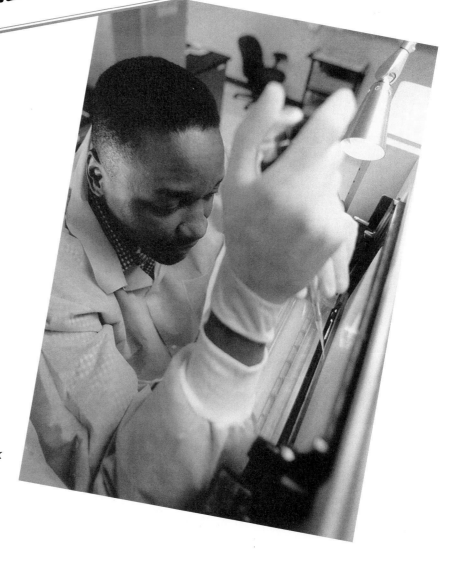

Using new methods of analysis, a specialist in the laboratory of the New York City Medical Examiner's office prepares DNA samples.

10
The Greasy Overalls

Detective work? A tough job, yes, but the scientific laboratory is coming to the aid of the crime investigator.

Trace evidence alone, collected by detectives, may not convict. But if it's recovered, it will often corroborate other evidence gathered during an investigation by lab experts. Hair is an example of a kind of physical evidence in many crimes. It can provide strong corroborative evidence to place someone at a crime scene. So during an autopsy, hair samples are collected routinely from the victim of a suspicious death. Who knows how useful those samples may prove later?

Human hairs are especially important in cases involving personal contact, such as rape and homicide. Hair, blood, and semen are most often the physiological evidence associated with crime.

Forensics is the use of scientific methods to catch criminals. A brilliant forensic scientist can work wonders in the most difficult cases. Among the best known was Edward O. Heinrich(1881–1953), a chemist whose crime lab at Berkeley used the most up-to-date scientific technology of his day. He was called in when the police failed after several weeks to find three armed men who had tried to rob a train in Oregon. They had dynamited the mail car and killed three of the train crew but fled without stealing anything.

A prolonged hunt for bits and pieces of evidence brought in only a revolver and a pair of greasy blue denim overalls. Was that all? What could it prove? Maybe that wizard Heinrich might find a clue. The overalls were sent to him. He put every stitch of the overalls under his microscope, including samples of the grease and debris from the pockets.

The result: he astonished the police by writing up a full description of the overall wearer they should be hunting for. He was a left-handed lumberjack from the logging camps of the Pacific Northwest, a man with light brown hair who rolled his own cigarettes and was fussy about his appearance. He was 5 feet 10, weighed about 165 pounds, and was in his early twenties.

How Heinrich deduced all this from his examination of the greasy overalls is told by Colin Evans in his *Casebook of Forensic Detection.*

> Heinrich was matter-of-fact. Because the pockets of the left side were more heavily worn than those on the right, and because the garment buttoned from the left, it was reasonable to assume that the wearer was left-handed. Chips of Douglas fir, common to the forests of the Pacific Northwest, were found in the right pocket, such as might be collected by a left-handed lumberjack standing with that side nearest the tree. Shreds of loose tobacco in both pockets were an obvious indicator of smoking preference.
>
> Simple measurement of the overalls gave Heinrich a good idea of the owner's build and height, while a pocket seam yielded several neatly cut fingernail parings, somewhat incongruous for a lumberjack unless he was fastidious about his appearance. A single strand of hair clinging to one button was light brown in color; the level of pigmentation suggested someone in his early twenties.
>
> In addition, Heinrich found one other clue that previous investigators had totally overlooked. Tucked into the bottom of a long, narrow pencil pocket was a tiny wad of paper. It had obviously undergone numerous washings with the overalls and was blurred beyond all legibility, but by treating it with iodine, Heinrich was able to identify it as a registered-mail receipt numbered 236-L.
>
> The Post Office traced the receipt for fifty dollars to one Roy D'Autremont of Eugene, Oregon, who together with his twin brother, Ray, and another brother, Hugh, had not been seen since October 11, the date of the train holdup. Inquiries about Roy revealed that he was left-handed, had often worked as a lumberjack, rolled his own cigarettes, and was very mindful of his appearance. . . .

Just plain soil may turn out to be the key to the solution of a crime. Crimes often occur under conditions where an amount of soil is transferred. Soil is a very rich and complex mixture—mineral grains derived from rock over eons of weathering or decayed organic matter of plants, as well as particles created by human activity. Soil may contain bits of paint, glass, concrete, asphalt, pollutants from factories, tire-rubber abradings, and still other trace evidence. In

The Korean Rope

"Every contact leaves a trace" is a principle detectives have gone by for nearly a hundred years. It's the root of forensic science. For example, in 1983 in Nebraska a thirteen-year-old schoolboy vanished. When his body was found a few days later, it was bound with rope. The rope was so unusual nobody recognized the type. All manufacturers in the United States and abroad were checked, with no results. A suspect the police were led to several months later insisted he was innocent. But in a duffel bag he owned, police found a piece of rope. Lab analysis compared it to the rope used to tie up the young victim. It was exactly the same, a very rare kind made only for the military in Korea. The suspect's scoutmaster had brought it back from there.

it may also be found fragments of plants that have yet to decay, as well as living microorganisms.

Investigators on the crime scene may find soil samples on the shoes or clothing or other things belonging to a suspect, as well as on the victim. When a victim has been killed in one place, and the body dumped in another place, soil evidence found on the victim may help prove where the murder took place.

In one rape-homicide case, a suspect was arrested shortly after the crime was reported. His clothing and his work boots were stained with mud. He was muddied, he said, because he had fallen in his own yard, which was just two blocks away from the scene of the crime.

Detectives took mud samples from the disturbed ground near the victim's body and, as controls, samples from other areas nearby, as well as on the path leading from the suspect's yard to the site of the crime. Laboratory examination of all the samples showed a high degree of similarity between samples taken from the shoes and clothing of the suspect and samples from the area around the body. The control samples were shown to be different in a significant degree. These findings together with other physical evidence helped to obtain a conviction.

Using special labeled bags, a policeman removes materials found in the apartment of a murder victim. A forensic scientist may find valuable clues to the identity of the killer in these samples.

11
Fingerprints, Millions of Them

One day in Miami a young cop stopped a green Volkswagen headed the wrong direction on a one-way street. The driver leaped out and ran down an alley. The cop chased him but the fugitive turned around, whipped out a revolver, shot the cop dead, and ran on. Squads of police searched buildings, streets, and fields on foot, with dogs, and by helicopter. They stopped dozens of suspects—and failed to find the killer.

A recently installed computer system is what nabbed the killer. Fingerprints lifted from the Volkswagen were fed into the machine. The computer instantly compared the fingerprints with hundreds of thousands on file. Within minutes the machine spit out the name of the car thief. The killer was convicted and sentenced to death.

The rapid pace of modern technology has had a dramatic effect upon police work. The Automated Fingerprint Identification System (AFIS) can scan and digitally encode fingerprints so that they can be subject to high-speed computer processing. Before police had that technology, they were usually limited to matching crime scene fingerprints against those of known suspects. Now a single, scarcely visible fingerprint from a crime scene can be searched against an entire file's print collection.

Fingerprinting is at the heart of modern criminal identification. From the beginning of police work, a foolproof method of identification has been sought. Back in 1883 a French police expert, Alphonse Bertillon, made the first systematic attempt at personal identification. His system relied on a detailed description of the suspect, combined with full-length and profile photographs and a system of precise body measurements called anthropometry.

That system was used for about twenty years, until it became clear the results were unreliable. It was found that the measurements of two people could sometimes be practically the same, and their pictures hardly told apart. What doomed Bertillon's method was the development of fingerprinting around the same time.

The modern idea of fingerprinting was introduced in 1880 when Henry Fauld, a Scottish doctor working in a hospital in Japan, published his view that fingerprints might be a means of identification. He told how a thief had left his fingerprints on a whitewashed wall. Comparing that print with those of a suspect, he found they were quite different. Soon after, another suspect was picked up; his prints did match those on the wall. Shown that evidence, the thief confessed.

Fauld was sure he had the answer. He offered to set up a fingerprint bureau at his own expense for the British police, but they preferred to stick to the Bertillon system. It was extensive research done by the British scientist Sir Francis Galton that changed the picture. He established that fingerprints were not inherited, that even identical twins had different patterns, and that prints remain unchanged from year to year. (Egyptian mummies have been found with their prints intact.) He laid the basis for a classification system, putting the most commonly observed features into three groups: arches, loops, and whorls. His book, *Finger Prints,* was published in 1892.

The next step was to work out a more detailed classification system capable of containing innumerable prints in a logical sequence, so that the files could be easily searched. Others refined Galton's system until Sir Edward Henry completed the task in 1897. He established five basic patterns, adding fonted arches to Galton's three groups and dividing loops into two classes.

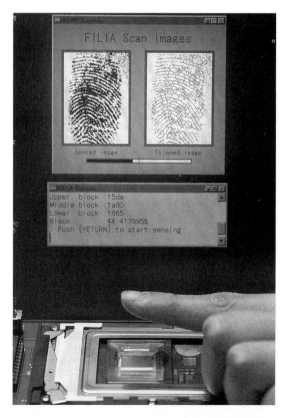

Today most English-speaking countries use some version of Henry's system. In the United States, New York City in 1901 was the first to make systematic use of prints. But not until 1912, in a historic ruling of the Supreme Court of Illinois,

New technology developed in Japan uses a microchip to identify fingerprints. On the monitor screen at left is the fingerprint image itself. At right is its computerized thinned image, which helps identification. The chip, shown beneath the finger, can identify a fingerprint in half a second with an accuracy level of 99 percent or more.

did judges sanction the admissibility of fingerprint evidence and uphold the right of experienced technicians to testify as experts. The accused was convicted and hanged.

Within a few years fingerprinting was being used in all major cities. The Federal Bureau of Investigation (FBI) began to build a collection of prints that is now the largest in the world. The total number of prints in the FBI file today is probably around 200 million, with thousands of print cards added daily. The files contain mostly the prints of arrested people, aliens, government job applicants, and military personnel. Some people voluntarily submit their fingerprints for personal identification reasons. Through a service called the International Exchange of Fingerprints, the FBI can exchange identification data with the law enforcement agencies of some eighty foreign countries.

Fingerprints are often found at crime scenes, whether the crime is larceny, burglary, rape, homicide, or whatever. Print comparisons help to catch fugitives and to determine whether a suspect has been arrested before. They are useful in identifying bodies, victims of amnesia, missing persons, and the victims of such mass disasters as earthquakes and tornadoes.

There are still other individualizing patterns that help identify people, such as palm prints and bite marks. Hospitals have long used the footprints of infants for that purpose. Still other markings and patterns include ear prints, lip prints, tattoos, and any other markings that give clues to a person's identity.

How are fingerprints taken from a crime scene? Friction ridges on the fingers contain sweat pores. Sweat mixed with other body oils and dirt produces fingerprints on smooth surfaces. Fingerprint experts use powders and chemicals to make such prints visible. However, it's almost impossible to determine the age of those impressions. At trials defendants often try to explain away evidence that these prints were found at the scene of the crime by testifying that yes, they were at that scene, but not at the time of the crime.

You'd think that with fingerprint evidence so convincing, criminals would always wear gloves. But Thomas McKenna, a detective with decades of experience on the New York City police force, says many lawbreakers don't have sense enough to wear gloves. The big-time guys—like the safecrackers—do wear gloves. But burglars? "All they want to do is get in, grab what they can, and get out. . . . The average burglar is dumb as shit. The average murderer? Why do they always still have the gun on them when they get caught? If they had any brains, they'd throw the gun away. But no!"

12
What DNA Proves

In March 2000 a man suspected in a series of sexual assaults in New York City was charged with rape after his DNA, recovered from a knife he had been stabbed with during an assault months before, linked him to two of the crimes. Detectives collected samples of the rapist's DNA from blood on the knife.

You've probably heard of DNA. Those letters stand for *d*eoxyribo*n*ucleic *a*cid. It's one of the two types of nucleic acid that the nucleus of every cell in our body has. DNA forms the building blocks of life. It dictates our hair color and eye color and everything else about our physical makeup.

Large chunks of DNA are universal. This is why each of us has the same body parts and organs. But some sections of DNA vary from person to person. Scientific analysis of those segments can show whether a partial strand of DNA could have come from a given individual.

The discovery of DNA goes back to 1868. Research continued—but slowly. The major breakthrough in understanding how DNA works came about in the early 1950s, when two scientists, Francis Crick and James Watson, deduced its structure. They found that DNA is an extraordinary molecule that carries out the task of controlling the genetic traits of all living cells, plant and animal. In 1984 Dr. Alec Jeffreys, an English scientist, perfected the means whereby identifiable genetic markers could be developed on an X-ray film as a kind of bar code and then compared with other DNA specimens. In 1986, called in to help on a murder investigation, he proved that a mentally retarded boy of seventeen who had confessed to the killing of two teenage girls was innocent; he had made up his confession. The boy was the first accused murderer to be cleared as a result of DNA typing.

DNA typing was declared acceptable as evidence in an American trial that

A medical service technician uses a computerized bar code reader to track batches of DNA samples.

same year. In that case DNA tests made on some samples of the blood and semen of an accused serial rapist served to convict him. Since then, DNA evidence has become widely accepted in courts across the country.

In criminal investigations the specimens are usually blood from the victim, from the accused, or any sample from the crime scene such as hair, bloodied clothing, or a semen stain in a case of rape. If such samples match the sample of the accused's blood, it is very strong evidence. Scientists estimate that the odds of any two people having the same DNA is somewhere around one in several billion. Ongoing research may modify this calculation someday. But as the twentieth century ended, DNA typing was valued as the most significant forensic development since the discovery of fingerprints.

DNA can be found almost anywhere. Criminals leave blood when breaking and entering, shed hair and skin cells in fights, deposit saliva on glasses, leave sweat stains in headbands. Enough DNA can be extracted from only a few cells to identify the person they came from. And there is considerable crossover. People who commit serious crimes often have convictions for petty crimes in their record. So if their DNA is entered into a database early, it may enable the police to prevent or solve serious crimes.

In 1998 the Federal Bureau of Investigation opened a national DNA database that it expected to significantly reduce the incidence of rape and other crimes by helping to catch repeat offenders early. That national database consists of the databases operated by all fifty states. They were unified by common methods and software designed by the FBI. This made it possible to compare DNA samples for a suspect on a crime scene in one state with all the others in the national system.

The blood or other samples taken from individuals are retained by the states in what are called DNA banks. Access to the DNA banks is permitted only for law enforcement purposes, with a $100,000 fine for unauthorized disclosures. The states differ on the types of offenses for which DNA profiles should be taken, though all agree that they should be taken for sexual crimes. The chief of the FBI forensic sciences unit believes that by sometime in the early twenty-first century, all felonies will be covered.

DNA Danger

Although forensic experts are delighted to have DNA databases as tools of their trade, civil libertarians are not so thrilled. They fear that the DNA database, which started out with sex offenders, may be extended to include everyone, giving elites the power to control "unruly" citizens. A bioethicist, Dr. Eric Juengst, who is a member of the FBI's DNA Advisory Board, warned that "as a society we have to learn how to control powerful tools of all kinds, like nuclear power."

In New York City the police commissioner and the mayor in 1999 proposed taking DNA samples from everyone arrested in the city, from subway turnstile jumpers on up, so career criminals could be locked up. The mayor also said he'd have "no problem" with DNA testing and fingerprinting of all newborn babies. He saw no reason why people should be afraid of being identified. Barry Scheck, a law professor and member of the FBI panel on DNA issues, warned that this invasion of privacy at birth "could be a step toward a total surveillance society."

Others point out that DNA sampling, done by collecting saliva, is not quite the same as taking fingerprints. There is a huge difference. Fingerprints can't be used for any purpose other than identification. DNA samples provide the government with extraordinary amounts of personal genetic information that could be misused. Such data could leak into the hands of insurance companies to identify those at risk for genetic diseases.

13
Bullets with Signatures

A street shooting takes place, and two detectives are called to the crime scene. A patrolman on duty reports he has no suspect in custody. All he has under a white sheet is the body of a small-time crack dealer everyone in the neighborhood knows.

The detectives learn that the victim was shot twice as he walked into a liquor store. One of the wounds was a "through-and-through," that is, the bullet passsed all the way through the victim's body. So the detectives try to trace the flight of that bullet. Finding a bullet could be worth a lot if a gun is recovered. If the forensics lab can match the bullet with the gun, it may be all the evidence needed.

Figuring out the direction the bullet took after leaving the victim's body, a detective digs into a chipped panel on the wall near the store's entrance and finds a single bullet slug.

At the police crime lab, a ballistics expert takes over the bullet. His is the science that deals with the motion of projectiles and the conditions affecting that motion—in other words, the study of firearms and bullets. Handguns go back to A.D. 1200. By the sixteenth century engineers realized that a spiral groove etched into the gun barrel would give a spin to the bullet, thus making its flight more stable and improving the aim. That groove—called rifling—leaves the distinctive marks known as striations on the bullet. This is the basis of ballistics research.

Not to get too technical, let's say firing a gun leaves a mark, or "signature," on the bullet. Two bullets fired from the same gun have identical groove impressions and marks. The ballistics expert matches these for a positive or negative identification.

Not only the barrel but other parts of a gun have individual characteristics. And the use and wear of a firearm add still more to the weapon's individuality.

Think back to how fingerprint variations can serve as a key to human identification. So too can minute random markings on surfaces make inanimate objects differ from one another. Scratches, nicks, breaks, and wear permit the examiner to connect a bullet to a gun. But the high rate of shootings—among the most serious crimes committed in our society—has pushed ballistics experts to go beyond the comparison of bullets.

Firearms are used in more than 60 percent of all homicides, more than 20 percent of all assaults, more than 35 percent of all robberies, and in almost half of all suicides. The experts need to know how all kinds of firearms operate; how to restore obliterated serial numbers on weapons; how to detect and

Bullets and firearms are tested at police department ballistics labs like the one shown here.

characterize gunpowder residues on hands, on clothing, and around wounds; and how to estimate muzzle-to-target distances.

Complicating the ballistic lab's difficulties is the fact that there is almost no limit to the number of different makes and models of firearms—including not only the familiar pistols, automatic handguns, shotguns, and rifles but such weapons as machine guns, artillery, and many variations of homemade weapons too.

One gun—no. 997126, a 12-shot, 9-millimeter Jennings automatic—has been linked to as many as thirteen crimes, including the murder of two people and the wounding of at least three others in Brooklyn, New York.

From the factory in California, the gun was shipped to a Nevada distributor, who sold it to a licensed wholesaler in Ohio. Then a pawnshop in Georgia bought it and resold the gun to a Georgia woman. She was fronting for a man barred from purchasing firearms because of a previous felony conviction. He carried the weapon to New York, where it was sold illegally to a parolee, a member of the Bloods gang.

The gun was used to kill a sixteen-year-old reputed member of the Crips gang. It was used again and again, killing or wounding other victims. When the Bloods gang member was arrested after shooting a policeman, police technicians used a computer at their ballistics lab to match the slugs recovered from each of the earlier shootings. They worked with a computerized database to match marks on casings of bullets fired in widely distant places. More than 200,000 guns are traced by this means in America each year.

14
Blood and Poison

Bloodstains occur very often in crimes of the most violent kind—homicides, assaults, rapes. During a struggle between the attacker and the victim, blood may stain the clothing of one or the other or both. Because in theory no two people except for identical twins can be expected to have the same composition of blood factors, a bloodstain becomes critical evidence.

The serological lab, which deals with reactions and properties of serums, is called upon to determine whether a bloodstain matches the blood of a victim or a suspect. The serologists' technology can tell them whether it is human or animal blood, what its blood group classification is, and its breakdown and composition.

It's difficult enough to do this with whole blood, but what makes it more troublesome is the fact that practically all blood evidence is received in the form of dried stains. As the blood dries, some of its characteristic blood factors are destroyed, and as the stain continues to age, that destruction slowly extends to other factors. Successful identification takes time, money, and brainpower.

After finding out whether a stain is indeed blood, and whether it is animal or human blood, investigators go on to determine the blood group and the sex of the person whose blood was spilled. Great care must be taken to collect blood in the proper way, for it is one of the most reliable and informative types of evidence.

The testing system used is very sensitive, requiring only minute samples. It is possible to obtain positive results on blood that has been dried for as long as fifteen years.

It's now known that as much as 80 percent of the population secrete their specific blood group in other bodily fluids, such as saliva. As serological research advanced, it became possible to identify some three hundred blood-group systems. But the effort to develop some kind of "blood fingerprint" slowed down when DNA typing proved so successful.

Another type of lab used in criminal investigations is the toxicology lab, which deals with poisons and their effects. Suppose someone is found dead with no apparent cause—no gunshot or knife wound, no crushing blow. The forensic toxicologist can determine whether a poison is present and what that poison is. The lab examines samples from vital organs, blood or urine, food, drink, and the suspected poison itself. The lab's caseload reflects the popularity of drugs that are abused in the community. Thousands die every year from the intentional or unintentional use of drugs Many innocent lives are lost because of the erratic or uncontrollable behavior of people who are under the influence of drugs.

Don't assume automatically that these injuries or deaths are the result of the wide use of illegal drugs. Alcohol, for instance, a *legal* over-the-counter drug, is the most heavily abused drug in Western countries. In the United States, in a given year, more than 17,000 automobile deaths and 40 percent of all traffic deaths were alcohol-related. Some 2 million people a year wind up in the hospital because someone at the wheel has been drinking. No wonder forensic toxicologists expect to be asked almost daily to determine the presence of alcohol in the body.

Once upon a time poisoners did their dirty work in almost perfect safety. They knew there was no way to detect poison in the body of their victim. Poisoning as a way of getting rid of rivals in love, political enemies, or business competitors, or to settle grudges, was "the thing." So popular a killing device led to the rise of professional poisoners who for a good price were hired by the rich or sometimes by the royal family to "take care of" someone who stood in the way or had gotten out of hand.

The problem of how to detect arsenic was solved in 1836 when James Marsh, a London chemist, invented a way of detecting even the smallest amount of arsenic. His test, now refined, is still in use. Today's toxicology chemists have to deal with much more than arsenic. There's strychnine and cyanide and a vast number of industrial and agricultural chemicals that can do harm. But poisoning in cases of homicide is now quite rare.

15
No Two Write Alike

When Hanna Sulner, one of the world's leading authorities on disputed documents, died in 1999, her life story reminded us of how brilliant and dramatic such a career can be. Often, of course, it deals with routine things, like the petty crime of forgery. A blank check is stolen and then written out for five hundred dollars. The thief forges the signature and cashes the check at his neighborhood bank. The victim guesses who the forger is, and the police search the man's apartment, finding a letter with what seems to be a matching signature. The forensic documents lab examines both signatures and determines that the signature on the check is the same as the writing found in the suspect's home.

The lab can do more: it can identify typewriting, inks, paper, and even writing left on a charred paper by putting it under a high-power microscope. The experts try to answer not only the question of who wrote a particular specimen but also the question of whether a document is the real thing—that is, what it purports to be, someone's diary or letter or notebook.

Mostly such labs deal with fraud investigation. But disputed document analysis can play an important role in all facets of crime detection, including homicide, contested wills, kidnapping, suicide, embezzlement, breaches of contract, extortion, and robbery. A well-equipped documents lab will have such items as magnifying lenses, stereomicroscopes, infrared microscopes, microcomparators, photographic devices, special lighting equipment, chemical reagents, and even more.

Hanna Sulner's story shows how a documents expert masters the science and the uses she puts it to. At the age of sixteen, Hanna studied with her father, a professor and pioneer in handwriting analysis who settled in Budapest after

Hanna and Laszlo Sulner display the microfilm of forged documents that Hungary's Communist regime used to frame Cardinal Mindszenty of crimes he never committed.

World War I. He won a reputation as Eastern Europe's leading expert on questionable documents. Hanna went on to study criminology and to teach in the law school of the University of Budapest. After her father died in 1944, Hanna became Hungary's chief documents expert for the courts, the police, and the military.

Laszlo Sulner joined her office in 1946, and they were married a year later. Gradually they were drawn into the Hungarian Communist government's attempt to discredit Cardinal Mindszenty, an outspoken opponent of the Communist regime. Under great pressure from the Communists—cooperate or be hanged!—the Sulners forged incriminating documents either in the cardinal's hand or bearing his signature. They used (or misused) a technique Hanna's father had invented for comparing handwritings. It made it possible to copy letters and words from one document and rearrange them into a new, incriminating one.

The cardinal was charged with treason and illegal monetary transactions. He was sentenced to life imprisonment. Before the trial ended, the Sulners fled to Vienna, denounced the trial as a farce, and displayed microfilm of the forged documents they had worked on. (The cardinal was freed because of ill health several years later, and he survived until 1975.)

A year after the trial, Mr. Sulner died in Paris. Hanna was convinced he had been poisoned by Communist agents. Soon after, Hanna came to New York to resume her career. She testified in more than 1,000 cases throughout the country—rarely for the losing side. As often happens in trials, expert witnesses are called to testify for opposing sides. Once, when Hanna testified against three rival experts in a dispute over a will, she convinced the jury that what seemed to be an authentic signature had been forged. How? By showing that the dots over three *i*'s were misplaced.

Comparison of written documents was one of the forms of evidence that helped convict Bruno Hauptmann of kidnapping and killing the Lindbergh baby in 1932.

The experts can determine the make and model of a typewriter used to prepare a typed document. Vertical misalignment in certain characters may be traced to a particular typewriter. If documents are burned or water damaged, whether for innocent or guilty purposes, the experts can restore them well enough to read them. They can even uncover the meaning of indented writing found on a paper pad after the top sheet has been removed.

All sorts of documents reach the crime lab for examination—checks, letters, driver's licenses, wills, contracts, passports, petitions. And experts may

Facsimiles of handwriting used as evidence in the Lindbergh kidnapping case. At top is Hauptmann's signature on an auto registration card at the bureau of motor vehicles. That signature is photographically enlarged just below. The uncannily similar signature just below that was pieced together using facsimiles of circled letters from the ransom note, bottom. Expert comparison of the documents helped convict the accused kidnapper.

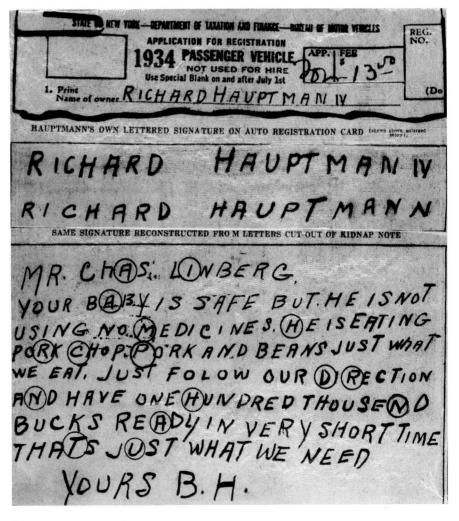

Hitler's Secret Diaries

One of the greatest publishing events in history was announced in 1981. It was the discovery of secret diaries kept by Adolf Hitler, the Nazi dictator of Germany who caused the most destructive war the world has suffered. A reputable German publisher said it had received sixty handwritten volumes of Hitler's diaries from a collector of Nazi memorabilia for which it had paid $4.8 million.

Only after the news broke did the publisher submit the diaries to "experts" for authentication. When they gave the diaries their stamp of approval, publishers abroad offered to buy foreign rights. A British historian was asked to review the documents and he too pronounced them authentic.

But all these approvals came tumbling down when forensic scientists in a West German police laboratory examined the documents. They found that the paper used in the diaries contained a substance, a paper-whitening agent, that had not been developed until nearly ten years after World War II and the death of Hitler. And chemical analysis of the inks used in the writing showed they were less than twelve months old.

It turned out that a Konrad Kujau, a petty swindler, had forged the diaries and fooled those first "experts." He was sentenced to four and a half years in prison. But how much damage was done to the reputations of the publisher, his experts, and the historian?

Konrad Kujau, at his trial in Hamburg, Germany, in 1984

uncover not only paper documents but other markings—on walls, windows, doors, or any other objects.

The general belief of documents experts is that no two people write exactly alike. There may be strong resemblances between them—say, a general style, perhaps learned at school. But eventually a person's writing takes on deeply set shapes and patterns that make it different from all others. Even when there is a strong effort to disguise the writing, some of the peculiarities continue to show up. These traits are what the documents expert looks for.

16
Secrets and Lies

Does it trouble you to tell a lie? Or can you carry it off without anyone suspecting? When a suspect is picked up for questioning, the way he or she responds can be terribly important.

Lie detector tests may help convict the guilty and clear the innocent. The device used, called a polygraph, seeks to identify deceit. The theory behind the test is that lying is stressful. If the subject lies in response to a question, that stress is detected and recorded on the polygraph machine. It monitors several of the subject's physiological functions—breathing, pulse, and perspiration—printing out the results on graph paper. The graph can show exactly when in the questioning period stress occurred. If the period of greatest stress lines up on the graph paper with the critical questions, it is presumed that's when the subject was lying.

The results are controversial. Some say attaching the gadget itself can induce stress and therefore yield faulty results. Joel Hirschhorn, a criminal defense attorney in Miami, said, "I've seen people pass the examination who should have flunked, and I've seen people fail the test they should have passed." Honest people are most vulnerable because they are not used to having their integrity challenged. Their breathing, pulse, and respiration may change, although they are completely innocent.

It would take a polygraph examiner with a solid background in either psychology or physiology to do accurate screening. How many are qualified?

Some courts won't accept polygraph results because "too much depends on nonscientific matters." But even though a court may not admit polygraph analysis into testimony, the accused, before trial, sometimes take the test voluntarily and, when presented with the results, decide to cut their losses and confess. Natale Laurendi, the star lie detector expert for the New York City police department for many years, played a vital role in such cases as the Wylie-Hoffert "career girls" murders in 1963. Working with detectives, he used his tests to help free a wrongfully convicted defendant and convict the real killer. In such cases, lie detector tests are valued as a good investigative tool for the defense, the prosecution, and the courts.

Can people be identified solely by the sound of their voice? The notion that this was possible led a scientist at Bell Telephone Laboratories to develop the sound spectograph. He believed that because the parts of the body used in speech—tongue, teeth, larynx, lungs, and nasal cavity—vary so much in size and shape among people, it would be impossible for the voices of any two persons to be exactly alike.

The spectograph machine obtains two kinds of voiceprints: bar prints and contour prints. The first are used for identification, the second for computerized filing.

The inventor claimed that a voice never changes throughout life. Other experts differ. They say our bodies and therefore our voices change with age. And the way we speak may change if we move, say, from New England to the South and pick up the accent of that region.

American courtrooms have been slow to accept voiceprints as evidence. But as with the lie detector, the police use it with suspects or witnesses and find that the results may lead to the capture of criminals. Experimental studies have shown a 99 percent rate of success with voiceprints. Professionals impersonating a voice have been able to defeat the system only 1 percent of the time. Yet if someone faces imprisonment or execution, a 1 percent error rate can be disastrous.

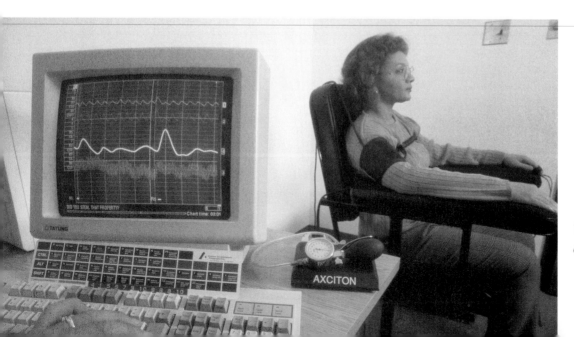

Taking a lie detection test

17 Eyewitnesses and Identification

An auto accident occurs on your street corner just as you are waiting for the traffic light to change. Two other people are standing there by you. Questions arise: Who is to blame for the crash? Which driver? Who was driving which car? What color and make were the two cars?

When such a case comes to court sometime later, and you and the other two witnesses are summoned to testify, chances are the three of you will differ on the details of what you saw. It may make the evidence confusing and contradictory.

Yes, eyewitness testimony is notoriously fallible. Yet identification is vital in many cases that reach the courts. Sometimes, when a suspect is brought in on the charge of raping a number of women over a period time, the several victims will fail to agree on identification—and not because anyone is lying or trying to cover up something. For what an eyewitness sees depends on many variable, inconstant factors, such as:

- eyesight
- climatic conditions
- visibility and illumination
- facial or bodily peculiarities and the possibility that those peculiarities may be duplicated in other persons
- ability of the witness to describe accurately the mannerisms by which he or she is able to tell the particular person apart from others of similar build
- the ability of that person to retain a clear mental image of the person he or she has seen

- the length of time between the witness seeing the suspect and the identification lineup
- the possibility of external influences (photos, newspaper descriptions, conversations with other witnesses, etc.)
- the actual conditions under which an identification lineup is conducted

That all has to do with living persons. What about the dead?

When a body is found, detectives will ask at once, who is it? The fact is, the majority of murder victims are done in by people they know—husband, wife, lover, parent, child, rival, competitor. . . . So the answer to the "who" question may lead right to the killer.

That's why murderers often do their best to conceal their victim's identity. Remove all clothing, mutilate the face, strip off all belongings, hide the body or dispose of it. But how? Bodies are bulky, hard to manipulate. They may float in water, resist fire, smell bad. And they provide so many clues to identification: bone, teeth, birthmarks, tattoos, blemishes, on and on.

If the time of death can be determined, it can be an important lead to the solution of the crime. One of the standard indicators is rigor mortis, the stiffening of the muscles, which usually sets in about three hours after death and takes about twelve hours to affect the whole body. After thirty-six hours the process reverses itself and the body becomes soft and supple again. Another indicator is lividity, or color change, which also develops in a regular sequence. Body temperature is a third factor in determining the time that death occurred. No indicator, say the experts, is wholly reliable.

The food a victim has eaten is another means of determining the time of death. The type of food eaten, the metabolic rate of digestion, fright, injury, pain can all influence digestion. But generally the average meal stays in the stomach for about two hours. Pathologists analyze the stomach contents, but it is often hard for them to come to a fixed conclusion. Experts can come up with divergent findings. Forensic pathologists, or coroners, provide evidence on both the time and cause of death. They may conclude, for example, that a victim found dead in the water did not die of drowning but of strangulation before entering the water.

In one case, reported worldwide, forensic photography was used in a reverse situation—to prove the identification of a dead suspect. He was Dr. Josef Mengele, the Nazi "Angel of Death" who had personally sent 400,000 Jews to their deaths during the Holocaust.

A forensics specialist superimposes a skull over the photograph of a victim's head in order to establish identification.

When World War II ended in Hitler's defeat, Mengele fled Germany for South America. Investigators hunted fruitlessly for him for many years. Then one day a German couple living in Brazil led police to the grave of a man buried under the name of Wolfgang Gerhard. But he was really Mengele, they asserted, dead from drowning in 1979 at the age of 67.

The coffin was opened, and an international team of scientists worked to discover the identity of the corpse. Using several forensic techniques, they decided the dead man was almost certainly Mengele. But what clinched the evidence was the use of video superimposition by a forensic anthropologist. He first marked more than thirty identifying features in the skull. Then, with two high-resolution video cameras, he shot pictures of the marked skull. Next he was able to make an exact match of known photographs of Mengele with a photo of the skull. It was reasonably certain, he concluded, that the bones in the coffin were those of Mengele.

Some still doubted that this was true. Final and irrefutable proof came years later, in 1992, when genetic material from the bones in the coffin was compared with samples taken from relatives of Mengele still living in Germany. The DNA analysis confirmed that the notorious mass-murderer had indeed died—unfortunately, without ever having been brought to justice.

This daguerreotype of Abraham Lincoln, taken in 1846 by N. H. Shephard, was the earliest known to exist until the discovery of an earlier daguerreotype.

Is It Young Mr. Lincoln?

Proving the identification of a homicide victim is one thing, but how can you prove that a very old picture that looks like Abraham Lincoln as a young man is really the future president?

A small oval daguerreotype of someone resembling the young Lincoln, made around 1843, turned up a few years ago. The earliest known picture of Lincoln, held in the Library of Congress, was made in 1846. It would be a major historical discovery to find an even earlier one.

The problem was handed to the head of a biomedical visualization lab. He had developed a process that feeds mathematical "facial maps" into a computer model and sifts the data for matches. To test the daguerreotype, he mapped it with three other Lincoln images and mixed them with three hundred other facial maps of white males. He got three matches—with the three other Lincoln images. He concluded this must be an authentic portrait of Lincoln.

18
Secrets in Old Bones

Crime laboratories help detectives with many services, several of them described in these pages. But there are still other specialized forensic services that crime investigators can draw upon. We've already mentioned forensic pathologists. They help establish who the victim is, what injuries there are, when they occurred, and how they were produced.

When only the skeletal remains of a victim are found, forensic anthropologists may be asked to help examine and identify them. A study of the bones may reveal their origin and the age, sex, and race of the victim. Although there is no face left, by analysis of the skeletal remains the anthropologist may be able to provide a facial reconstruction that an artist can sketch as a portrait for distribution in the hope that someone will recognize the victim.

What about the corpse of a victim found a considerable time after the crime was committed? Decay has set in and insects such as carrion flies infest the body. This situation brings forensic entomologists into play. They can identify the specific insects present and estimate by the development of the fly larvae how long the body has been left exposed—and thus help to determine the time of death.

Sometimes a body is found in such a state of decay or destruction that it is unrecognizable. That's when dental experts can help. Called forensic odontologists, they have only the victim's teeth to work with. Teeth, composed of enamel, are the hardest substance in the body. They outlast tissues and organs as the body decomposes. The nature of the teeth, their alignment, and their structure in the mouth offer evidence for pinning down the identity of the person. The dental remains of the victim can be compared with dental records, such as X rays and dental casts, and even a photograph of the suspected victim's smile. In assault cases bite marks might be found on the victim. The

Skeletons were found buried in Yekaterinburg, Russia, where Czar Nicholas II and his family and servants were executed after the Communists seized power in 1917. Forensic scientists examined the skeletons in 1998 to determine whether these were the remains of the royal family. It was concluded that the skeletons belonged to the czar, his wife, three of their daughters, and four servants.

odontologist is able to analyze those marks and compare them with the teeth structure of a suspect.

Several forensic scientists helped in 1999 to uncover evidence of a massacre that had occurred seventeen years before in a remote Mayan village of Guatemala. Army troops had rounded up 376 villagers and after torturing the men, women, and children, killed them with knives, machetes, bullets, and grenades. Such atrocities were common in the 1980s, reported the *New York Times,* "as the government, which had support from the United States, sought to crush rebel guerrilla groups."

When the thirty-six-year war ended in 1997, volunteer forensic anthropologists and other specialists, with the Guatemalan government's backing, came in to work at a few of the massacre sites. They gathered evidence from shattered bones, spent bullets, and domestic objects. They used many of the same techniques police use at crime sites. Americans and Guatemalans worked together, applying their experience as anthropologists, archaeologists, and odontologists to pick through the rubble of recent history to identify the victims and prove the extent and nature of the brutal killings.

Sadly, such tragedies occur so often that one forensic anthropologist, Dr. Clyde S. Snow, of Oklahoma, has investigated massacres in twenty countries in Latin America, Africa, the Balkans, and Asia.

But it is not only abroad that unidentified skeletons are found, possibly the victims of criminal assault. Every year about a million children under eighteen disappear in America. Most of them are gone only a short while. They are runaways or have been abducted by parents or strangers. Some are just lost.

When Mummies Speak

Archaeologists are trained, of course, to come up with answers to questions about prehistoric people, people who died thousands of years ago. Professor Elizabeth W. Barber has studied giant-sized mummies, wrapped in vivid textiles, found in tombs in far western China. These mute witnesses of ancient times, with their hollow eyes and shrunken skins, together with the artifacts buried with them, provide invaluable clues to the past. Examining all the evidence she finds, the way a police detective would, she builds a picture of how the prehistoric civilizations of Asia and Europe met in Central Asia, the greatest crossroads for early peoples and the spread of their languages and technology.

But you're unlikely to connect archaeology with criminal investigation. The skills of that profession prove useful when a buried body is unearthed. That means the soil layers have been disturbed and probably replaced in the wrong order. The forensic archaeologist studying such clues as minor ground undulations can provide a pretty good estimate of when the body was buried.

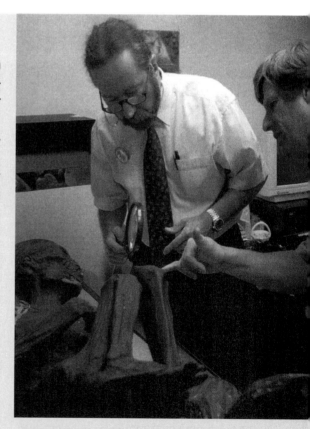

Two medical researchers examine a one-thousand-year-old female mummy from Peru.

Some, however, are the victims of murderous criminals, and in such cases forensic anthropologists may be called upon to help solve the crime. In the storage rooms of police stations all over America, there are human remains waiting for someone to identify them. David Hunt, an expert in skeletal biology at the Smithsonian's National Museum of Natural History, has worked with thousands of human remains—prehistoric, pre-Columbian, modern—over the past twenty years. A vast forensic database of skeletal measurements at the University of Tennessee helps him to analyze the gender and ethnicity of a subject. The information such experts come up with often proves useful to detectives.

Knowledge of the human mind is sometimes as important as knowledge of the human body in providing clues to the solution of a crime. That's why you often read of psychiatrists testifying at trials, for the defense or the prosecution. Their forensic specialty rests upon their knowledge of human behavior in situations both normal and abnormal. In criminal cases they evaluate behavioral disorders and determine whether the accused is competent to stand trial. Forensic psychiatrists who have made long-term studies of the behavioral patterns of criminals can aid detectives by providing a psychological profile of the kind of person who may have committed the crime in question.

PART THREE

Detective Work— Not on the Police Force

Allan Pinkerton started the most famous private detection agency in the nation.

19 The Pinkertons and the Molly Maguires

You are a father and your teenage daughter has been missing for several days.

You are a mother and your ex-husband has stopped paying family support and has moved to no one knows where.

You are a corporate executive and you suspect someone in the company has been selling trade secrets to a competitor.

You are an insurance company's claims expert and you feel that someone claiming injury is faking it.

What do you do? For personal reasons you do not wish to go to the police. Instead, you may decide to hire a private detective. There are thousands of them, found everywhere. Many operate on their own; others are members of large or small private investigative agencies.

The man who invented the profession of private detective was Allan Pinkerton. Born in 1819 in Scotland, he emigrated to America as a young man and settled near Chicago in 1842. He was a cooper by trade, earning a bare living at making barrels. One day he was called upon by a neighboring store-keeper to help trace a gang of counterfeiters and horse thieves. Putting together some clues, he was able to lead the police to their island hangout. That success, followed by others as an amateur "crook catcher," brought an offer to become Chicago's first police detective.

He didn't stay long on the job. Ambitious and talented, he quit to form his own private agency. He hired nine men as his "operatives," the term he preferred to "detective." The training he gave them was based on his belief that "the ends, being for the accomplishment of justice, justify the means used."

In practice that meant, if Pinkerton thought it necessary, his operatives wouldn't hesitate to kidnap. Or to lie. Or to pretend to be criminals when among them, and do whatever they did. James Horan, one of his biographers, described the Pinkerton methods:

> He taught them the art of "shadowing," of disguise, and of playing a role. His office often resembled the backstage of a theater, with Pinkerton demonstrating to an operative ready for assignment how to act like a "greenhorn" just off the boat, a bartender, a horsecar conductor, or a gambler. He kept a large closet in his private office filled with various disguises.

Pinkerton himself, tough, hard muscled, didn't hole up in his office giving orders to others. No, he mixed it up with the badmen, riding shotgun on stage coaches, foiling bank robberies, trailing outlaws through the Wild West, pursuing them even into the jungles of Central America.

As a youngster in Scotland, Pinkerton had been a militant radical, active in the Chartist movement, a movement in England that advocated better living and working conditions for factory workers. In America he continued for a time to side with the oppressed. For example, in 1859 he gave his friend John Brown, the abolitionist, critical help in transporting a band of runaway slaves to Canada.

Always on the lookout for whatever would improve his agency's work, Pinkerton embraced new technology. He used the telegraph to trace over great distances criminals on the run and photography to develop files of mug shots. He pioneered the use of women detectives, hiring them, he said, because they could better "worm secrets" out of men.

When Abraham Lincoln became president, he chose Pinkerton to create a military intelligence service. During the Civil War, Pinkerton uncovered Confederate spies operating behind the lines and in Washington.

Gradually Pinkerton built his agency into the largest one in the country. Its logo was a single unblinking eye and its slogan, "We Never Sleep." The eye symbolized the claim that Pinkertons saw everything, solved crimes by the power of their investigation, and prevented crimes by recognizing criminal behavior.

Toward the end of the nineteenth century, as the labor movement began to exert powerful pressure on the giant new corporations—in the railroads, the steel mills, the coal mines—the local police seemed unable to handle labor disputes. The Pinkerton agency became the source of hired (and often armed) men "to protect business property." The industrialists wanted help in keeping wages low, hours long, profits high, and unions out. Quickly the Pinkertons became known—and hated—as union busters. As labor disputes erupted all

Allan Pinkerton (left) with President Abraham Lincoln on a visit to a Union army camp during the Civil War

across the land, the Pinkertons were brought in to break strikes and safeguard scab workers, or workers who had been hired to replace other workers on strike. Pinkerton had made a radical switch in his philosophy—from his youthful defense of labor rights to the well-paid destruction of unions.

Pinkerton's most dramatic success with infiltration came when Franklin B. Gowen, the head of a Pennsylvania railroad and coal trust, hired his agency in 1870 to penetrate a militant young union and break it.

The miners union, called the Workingmen's Benevolent Association (WBA), embraced the largely immigrant workers of the coal industry. All workers, regardless of craft status, national origin, or religious background, were eligible to join. The union's policy was patient and peaceful negotiation with management; it strongly opposed any use of violence. And it did its best to protect miners from the terrible dangers of underground labor, which the mining companies did little to eliminate.

A tiny minority of miners, the Irish, discriminated against by the operators, who gave the best jobs to the English or Welsh miners, favored violence. That brand of protest, called "Molly Maguireism," had been known in the early nineteenth century in Ireland, where through rural secret societies it was used against landlords and their agents, the police and magistrates. The Mollys acquired that name because in Ireland they disguised themselves in women's clothing as they roved the countryside, dedicated to direct violent action against injustice on behalf of a mythical oppressed mother who had to beg for bread.

Here in America many Irish immigrants joined the Ancient Order of Hibernians (AOH), a peaceful fraternal society with lodges throughout the Northeast.

Gowen, a brilliant young lawyer, was familiar with the Pinkertons. His goal was to break the miners union. And his strategy was to smear the union with the Molly Maguire brush. He asked Pinkerton to send in a secret agent to spy on the union and the Mollys, supposedly only to stop the Mollys' violence.

Pinkerton gave one of his agents, James McParlan, a young Irish immigrant, the dangerous job of working undercover among the miners. The operative changed his name to James McKenna, got a job in a mine, and carefully worked his way into friendship with the Irish in the coal region. Within five months he was sworn into the AOH lodge. And when they saw he was one of the few among them who could read and write, they appointed him secretary.

A depression broke out in 1873. It was one of America's biggest and worst. It grew deeper until it had engulfed nearly all but the rich. With thousands of homeless men and women sleeping in the streets, and soup kitchens struggling to feed the hungry, business tried to preserve profits by cutting wages. Early in 1875 the mine owners, led by Gowen, announced a 20 percent wage cut. The union shut down the coalfields, and then owners launched a reign of terror. A band of hired vigilantes waylaid, ambushed, and killed militant miners.

But as the strike wore on, the miners' families came near to starvation. The owners reopened the mines and the desperate workers straggled back in. The union crumbled.

Bitterness and anger seized the Irish, who, after this humiliating defeat, were discriminated against and had trouble obtaining justice. When Irish went to court to remedy grievances they usually met delay, indifference, or hostility. So some—the Molly Maguires—resorted to violence for the quick settlement of scores. Policemen, pit bosses, a justice of the peace were shot down.

McParlan, as a trusted member of AOH, sometimes had advance knowledge of planned killings. He would then arrange for a secret squad of Pinkertons to be sent in. Their aim was to be present when a killing occurred, in order to collect eyewitness accounts and the physical evidence necessary for convictions.

After two and a half years inside the mining community, McParlan decided to quit and left the region. His written reports and other data he'd gathered were given to the prosecutors who were preparing the trials. He was asked to testify in court and at first refused. Then he changed his mind and appeared often as the chief witness. The trials of the Molly Maguires began in January 1876 and stretched out for more than two years. McParlan maintained that the AOH and the Molly Maguires were the same organization.

The outcome of the trials was the conviction and execution of twenty miners. Another twenty-six were sentenced to prison terms.

The historian J. Anthony Lukas, researching Pinkerton history, wondered how the deaths of such men affected the detective who had sent them to the gallows. "After all," Lukas wrote, "these were men with whom McParlan had lived for two and a half years, working in the mines, singing ballads, swapping yarns, and getting drunk. Did he feel even the slightest pang of regret at this betrayal of their confidences, or at their gruesome ends in white hoods, strangling in the hangman's noose? If he did, nowhere in his reports or letters, then or later, is it recorded."

The defendants were convicted on the evidence of a Pinkerton detective who was accused of being an agent provocateur. The state prosecutor was none other than Franklin Gowen himself—the corporate head whose aim was to crush the union. Most of the other prosecutors worked for railroads or mining companies.

As the labor historian Harold Aurand noted:

> The Molly Maguire investigations and trials marked one of the most astounding surrenders of sovereignty in American history. A private corporation initiated the investigation through a private detective agency, a private police force arrested the supposed offenders, and coal company attorneys prosecuted—the state provided only the courtroom and hangman.

This engraving depicts the Homestead Strike of 1892. Carnegie Steel hired armed Pinkertons to come in and break up the strike.

20 Cloak-and-Dagger Work Among the Corporations

By the 1930s the Pinkertons were operating as a sort of unofficial national police force. For until the Federal Bureau of Investigation (FBI) was created in 1908, America had no national police force. The Pinkerton agency was called on to investigate and solve interstate crimes beyond the reach of local and state police units. Expanding almost year by year, by 1965 it had 13,000 employees and 45 offices in the United States and Canada. In the 1990s Pinkerton had grown to 250 offices worldwide, with 50,000 employees. No longer in family hands, it had gone public. As the nineties ended, Pinkerton's was acquired by Securitas of Sweden, a giant private security agency. The new combined company would have 114,000 employees, operating in Europe, the Americas, and Asia.

Today the world's huge multinational corporations engage in corporate cloak-and-dagger work. They use covert operations, spies, and high-tech surveillance devices to find out what the competition is doing or to protect their own secrets from the competition.

Agencies like Pinkerton are banded together in the American Society for Industrial Security. In the late 1990s their total annual income had soared to more than $100 billion. Much of this comes from reliance by corporations on specialized agencies to deal with undercover skullduggery. The corporations spy on one another and try to win over informers among the key employees of the competition. The agencies do background checks on staff to see if they are living more lavishly than their income warrants. They provide training in basic security, such as making sure the employees do not leave a laptop computer full of confidential information on the next seat while they read the newspaper in some airport lounge. They sweep offices and phones for bugs at regular intervals and set up toll-free hot lines so employees can report anonymously on any suspicious activity. When mergers are in the offing, the agencies investigate potential partners, business rivals, and executives. Of course, anyone suspected of taking bribes or carelessly giving away critical information is watched closely.

With the rapid growth of technology, private investigative agencies are asked to protect software codes and customer lists from hackers who try to steal them.

The spying trade is quick to make use of electronic snooping gear. There are laser microphones that reconstruct conversations taking place inside a room from minute vibrations on windowpanes. Another device uses faint electromagnetic radiation emitted by a computer monitor to reproduce the screen.

But the old nineteenth-century practice of peddling agency services to bust unions has not died away. Only now it has assumed the more sophisticated forms the electronic age has made available. Some agencies have made

A variety of electronic monitoring equipment is displayed at a store called Spy World.

a specialty of offering help to companies fearing a unionization drive or wishing to break with unions already holding contracts.

More primitive thieving occurs too, with armed thugs breaking in to steal computer chips, which they sell to brokers who deal in them.

In the nation's capital, private investigators are used by either or both sides of political controversies. Their task is to search for embarrassing information to be leaked to the press or used as ammunition in congressional hearings. For example, when a tobacco company whistle-blower testified against his employer, a private snoop was paid to dig up dirt to discredit the witness.

One leading agency of this kind is Investigative Group International (IGI). Formed in 1994, within five years it had grown to a staff of one hundred full-time experts with offices in many major cities as well as abroad. Its staff includes not only lawyers but former police detectives, FBI and CIA agents, and TV reporters and producers.

David Samuels, who reported on IGI for the *New York Times*, wrote that "the power once held by J. Edgar Hoover—someone who worked behind the scenes, who knew all the secrets and exerted enormous influence on public affairs—has passed into the hands of private men."

A new twist in private investigative work occurred when the cold war between the Soviet Union and the West ended around 1990. Within ten years former CIA and KGB agents were working together as business partners to provide sensitive information to American corporations. (The KGB had been the Communist power's hated and feared intelligence agency.) Hundreds of out-of-work spies from the United States and Russia are now providing protection, intelligence, and political risk assessments to American companies as they seek to reach into markets abroad. These agencies not only provide information on business conditions and prospective partners but, when trouble threatens, help deal with kidnappings, fraud, theft, and extortion.

21 Going After the Mafia

As the twentieth century neared its end, *Time* magazine published a list of the one hundred "most influential business geniuses of the century." Odd as it seems, among those to whom the editors paid tribute was Charles "Lucky" Luciano. Who was he? And what was his great achievement?

Lucky Luciano was the man who united the blood-feuding gangsters of America into a centrally supervised criminal syndicate, which became known as the Mafia. And Luciano has gone down in the history of crime as the godfather of all godfathers.

Yes, Luciano used some of big business's methods to succeed. But his rise to the top of his criminal profession was based mostly on murdering lots of people. In 1936 Luciano was indicted on ninety counts of extortion and other crimes and sentenced to prison. In World War II the government went to him in prison to seek his influence in preventing work slowdowns on the mob-controlled shipping docks. Even behind bars he continued to hold leadership of the mob.

The Mafia itself had existed long before Luciano. (No one who belonged to it ever called it that. It was usually Cosa Nostra, or "Our Thing"!) Crime outfits with historical Italian-Sicilian roots were operating in several American cities by the late nineteenth century—and in so brutal a manner, wrote one historian, that "they made the Molly Maguires look like choirboys." Each family ruled over its own territory, often in bloody conflict with rival families over the control of criminal activities.

We hear far more about "crime in the streets" than about organized crime. Yet organized crime involves thousands of criminals who operate outside the control of government. The local core group may be known as the "Syndicate"

Charles "Lucky" Luciano, who came to New York from Sicily in 1906 and muscled his way to the top of organized crime. Early in his career, he was taken for a ride by rival thugs and left for dead on a Staten Island beach. Because of his extraordinary survival he was called "Lucky."

or the "Mob." What they all want is money and power—just like law-abiding businesses and citizens. Organized crime has its own standards and procedures, private and secret ones it creates for itself, changes when it sees fit, and administers ruthlessly.

Almost every American's life is affected by organized crime. Because it operates secretly, we can't realize how we are affected. The price we pay for a great many things and services we buy or use is often higher because of a conspiracy by organized crime to hike those prices. But we have no way of knowing that.

How come organized crime flourishes the way it does? Because it supplies a lot of people with goods and services they want—drugs, prostitution, the chance to gamble, desperately needed cash. The profits come from filling those needs.

Not only does organized crime satisfy these needs; it probably makes even bigger profits by extortion of both illegitimate and legitimate business. The Mob forces "protection" on enterprises of all kinds. The wholesale fish company can't unload its fish at the docks unless it pays off the Mob. The contractor finds that he can't finish work on a building unless he pays off the Mob. Sometimes the businessman finds he can survive only if he makes the Mob his partner. Exerting a strong grip on some trade unions, the Mob profits by extorting money from employers in exchange for labor peace.

Today the Mob controls many kinds of production and service industries and businesses. It also invests part of its illegal profits in legal enterprises. The racketeers have a steady flow of cash with which to invest in any business.

In recent years groups of people from other countries—Colombians, Cubans, Mexicans, Jamaicans, Vietnamese, Chinese, Russians, Filipinos, Nigerians—have emerged as rivals to the already established crime organizations in drug dealing as well as in other trades. Many of these enterprises know no ethnic or national boundaries. This makes it harder for investigators to identify them with precision. Theirs is a multibillion-dollar transnational business. Profits from drug trafficking alone run to some $200 billion to $300 billion a year.

Intensive detective work by local, state, and federal investigators has helped to gain some ground against organized crime. In the 1980s more than one thousand mafiosi were convicted in federal courts and sent to prison. The top leaders of four of the five New York Mafia families were convicted, and so were the leaders of families in Boston, Cleveland, Denver, Kansas City, Milwaukee, New Jersey, and St. Louis.

What helped mightily to make this accomplishment possible was a new strategy embodied in a 1970 statute devised by a Department of Justice attorney. The idea of the Racketeer Influenced and Corrupt Organizations Act (RICO) was to go after all the racketeering enterprises in a broad, sweeping manner. A related series of investigations was launched, aimed not just at the leadership but at the entire organization, top to bottom, including everything it had a hand in, every tangible asset the FBI could identify. RICO allows the law to seize homes, cars, and businesses purchased with profits from illegal enterprise. The officials hoped, when the law was through with it all, that there would be no one left within the criminal organization able to carry it on.

How was the RICO Act used? On so large a scale it consumed a large portion of the FBI's staff and energy. When the operation began in New York City in 1979, there were five families of the Cosa Nostra operating there: the Gambinos, the Genoveses, the Luccheses, the Colombos, and the Bonannos. Ten FBI organized crime squads were put on the job, with about 270 agents. They worked with one hundred New York City police officers and detectives.

Often detectives install bugs to help solve old crimes and sometimes prevent new ones. The electronics equipment required for this secret surveillance includes microphones, wiretapping paraphernalia, transmitters, receivers, tape recorders, playback units, closed-circuit television systems, and videotape machines. It's nice for law enforcement to have all this special technology handy. But these gadgets don't operate by themselves. It takes people to master their use, place them where they'll do the best job, and apply what is learned from them.

And such people must have the courage to take great risks—risks that come from missteps, miscalculations, or failures. For this type of work carries with it the possibility that your legs will be broken, your head smashed in, your body, punctured with bullets, encased in cement and dumped into a river.

Imagine what you might do if caught trying to place a bug under a Mafia man's bed? That happened to one FBI agent in New York. He bluffed his way into Sonny Red's apartment, posing as a house repairman. Working his magic to get through the man's door, he thought he'd see if placing a bug under his bed might do the job. He had slid himself under it when the bedroom door opened and in walked the man himself, just back from the bathroom.

"What are you doing here?" said Sonny Red. "Do what you gotta do, but I gotta have my sleep. Okay?" Then he got undressed, flopped down on his bed, and promptly fell asleep—with the agent still halfway under the bed. Quietly the agent slid free and left the apartment. He'd come back another time to put that bug where it would do the most damage.

Another incident that could have turned out tragically had a hilariously happy outcome for the crime fighters. The FBI had placed an informer, Vinnie De Penta of the Bonanno family, in charge of a business importing shipments of pasta that they hoped his people would want in on. Inside the business office, the agents had placed mikes and carefully concealed video cameras. The whole system was rigged to transmit everything at once back to the FBI office.

One day a Mafia wise guy, Frankie the Beast, dropped in to schmooze with De Penta. Somehow his eye spotted a video camera. Suspecting nothing, he said, "Hey, that's a great security system you got here. What did it cost you?" Trembling inside, but without losing his cool outside, De Penta replied it was actually a freebie. A couple of buddies had stolen it and put it in for him for no charge. "For nothing? Hey, that's great!" said Frankie. "Did you know Tommy DiBella [acting boss of the Colombos] is looking for a security system for his own house? And this one looks like it would be perfect!"

And that's what happened. FBI experts walked right through the front door of the mafiosi's home and installed the FBI cameras and mikes under the wise guys' noses.

Head shots of the Gambino crime family used in an exhibit during the trial of John Gotti in 1991

22
The Investigative Reporter

The skills, the insight, and the courage a good detective has are just what make a good investigative reporter—plus the ability to write well.

Not every journalist is an investigative reporter. A reporter may attend a city council meeting, take notes or tape what's said, then write the story. He simply takes the facts visible on the surface and edits them into a readable account.

But the investigative reporter, often on his or her own initiative, hunts for what someone wishes to conceal. How does it happen, for example, that local banks never provide mortgages for homes in a minority neighborhood? If, in seeking the answer, the reporter senses secrecy or evasion by bank officials, the next step is investigation. The reporter pulls together information from documents and from human sources, and eventually informs readers, viewers, and listeners about a practice that affects a large number of people, directly or indirectly.

Most of us are familiar with crime reporting. We read it or see it or hear it almost hourly. That kind of journalism, exciting as it sounds, can be routine. Usually it means hanging around in the dingy pressrooms close by police headquarters. In these pressrooms reporters monitor the police radio and respond to promising emergencies. If this is your job, you'd better be friendly with the detectives who can give you hot information about the latest gruesome killing or glorious arrest.

If you take the police side of the story, that's that. But some reporters challenge that side. Were those cops honest, competent? How about the lawyers and judges? Did they favor someone at the cost of justice? Did they overlook crimes you know occurred? An investigative reporter would want to know why the police or the district attorneys or the judges haven't achieved their stated goals. What stopped them from doing the work they're supposed to do?

Covering crime isn't glamorous. J. D. Mullan, who'd done it for years in Pennsylvania, wrote:

> There's nothing sexy about working crazy hours and sustaining your-self for days on Cheez-its and Coca-Cola from the cafeteria vending machines. There's nothing rewarding in running into dead ends, and getting burned by sources or having to write a correction. And after the lonely torture of writing is over, there's nothing more frazzling than arguing with some tin-eared editor who's convinced that your clever turn of phrase is really editorializing.

And yet sometimes a story comes along that makes you willing to put in fifteen-hour days and work on the weekends. "Maybe it's the pursuit of some injustice," Mullan says. Or "maybe it will crack the town wide open. . . . Whatever the case, it burns inside you, and you're possessed."

It's a job that means asking tough questions that people hate to hear and don't want to answer. It can take its toll. Investigative reporters can be threatened and shoved and spied on and sued—and sued by cops too, who don't like what you've said about them.

That burning desire to know, to find out, to learn what no one else has a clue to, can put you directly in danger. S. K. Bardwell, a Texas reporter, once had to spend several hours in an emergency room after she walked into a warehouse that firefighters hadn't taped off yet because it wasn't really burning—but that turned out to be full of poisonous gas. Her editor yelled at her, "Why in God's name did you get so close?" "Because I could," she said. And silently added, "Stupid."

Lynn Bartels, who covered crime in New Mexico for over a dozen years, did a superb investigation of the problem of drunken driving. The state had an appalling record for the problem, the worst in the nation. She found that prosecutors dismissed DWI charges or delayed acting until many months after a fatal crash.

In one case a convicted murderer on parole was arrested three times on drunken driving charges. Although police entered his name on a computer, nothing came up. Nowhere did they learn that he was free on bond for a heinous alcohol offense or that he was out of jail on special restrictions. No one had any idea that this was a man with a past. The system had failed, over and over again. And she wanted to find out why.

Top-rate investigative reporting produced a shocking newspaper series:

> We uncovered a driver who had at least 25—and possibly 41—arrests for driving while intoxicated. We rode with DWI officers and watched as drunken drivers stumbled and vomited and still maintained they had had nothing to drink. We sat in packed courtrooms and watched as inexperienced prosecutors and lousy judges allowed these same people to go free. We revealed how liquor interests controlled the legislature. We discovered that drunken drivers killed every 34 hours and that 261 people had died [as a result of drunken driving incidents] in 1991 in New Mexico.

At the next session of the legislature, important reforms were passed, many of them recommended by the investigative series of Lynn Bartels's newspaper. Within five months the state's Traffic Safety Bureau reported that drunken driving deaths had dropped an astounding 20 percent.

Gary Craig is an example of the investigative reporter who pursues a trail tenaciously in the hope of righting a wrong. Working for the *Rochester Democrat and Chronicle* in upstate New York, he heard of a woman some believed to have been wrongly imprisoned for many years for a murder.

In 1996 Craig began to examine police files and court transcripts of Betty Tyson's case. He found plenty of red flags. Ms. Tyson, a prostitute and heroin addict, had been picked up in a street sweep after the murder of an out-of-town businessman. It seemed a rogue detective had beaten confessions out of her and a teenage witness who said he saw her with the victim.

Craig discovered that the detective—now deceased—had been convicted

Betty Tyson is one of many prisoners who have been unjustly convicted but eventually freed because of the painstaking work of investigative journalists. Tyson spent half her life behind bars until Gary Craig secured her release.

Crime Busters at the Word Processor

Everybody knows what an investigative reporter is. He's the guy with the dangling cigarette, the grim visage, the belted trench coat, the snap-brim fedora. He slinks in and out of phone booths, talks out of the side of his mouth, and ignores other, lesser reporters.

He never had to learn his trade. He was born to it. He sprang from his mother's womb clutching a dog-eared address book and a set of pilfered bank records. He has an interminable list of contacts. His job consists largely of calling the contacts and saying, "Gimme the dope." The contacts, of course, always have the dope at their fingertips and are only too glad to part with it. He has all the time in the world to pursue sleazy characters through seamy intrigues. He appears in the city room only every two or three months to drop his copy on the desks of his astonished editors, mumble a few words, and disappear again into the night.

There is no such person. For one thing, he may be a she. For another, many general assignment reporters, political reporters, and feature writers—in print and broadcast journalism—wind up doing investigative reporting from time to time. In fact, any reporter who does the job well is already part investigator. Those who merely record the public words of people powerful enough or clever enough to attract the media's attention are publicists or stenographers; they are not journalists.

The only workable definition of an investigative reporter is a reporter who spends a lot of time doing investigations.

— From *Investigative Reporting*
by David Anderson and Peter Benjaminson

for faking evidence in one case and had been a defendant in civil suits accusing him of police abuse. He learned that Wayne Wright, the teenager, had confided to his family that he had lied on the witness stand. Although there was no physical evidence against her, the jury had convicted Ms. Tyson.

Craig researched the detective's history and found much to support claims of abusive conduct. He tracked two counselors who had been at the jail where Ms. Tyson was held after her 1973 arrest. They said she had had bruises on her arms and legs. He located Wayne Wright, whose confidence he gained after many long talks. Wright agreed to say on the record that he had lied on the stand after being beaten by the detective.

The result of nearly two years of investigation? Betty Tyson was freed in 1998—twenty-five years to the day from her arrest. "This is the sort of work we should be doing," Craig told the *New York Times*. "But I worry we're doing less of it than we used to."

But investigative journalism doesn't have to do only with exposing the bad, the harmful, the unjust. Jack Nelson, one of America's top reporters, found that out. Back in 1960 he won the coveted Pulitzer Prize for his coverage of the Milledgeville State Hospital in Georgia. It was then the nation's largest mental institution, with 12,500 patients and just 48 doctors. Conditions were terrible; it was a snakepit, a warehouse for humans.

Out of that experience came an important lesson in journalism. "Always follow up reports exposing bad conditions," he said, "with additional reports on proposals to reform or correct the conditions." Such reports demonstrate that the newspaper cares as much about reform as it does about an exposé. "Too often today," Nelson says, "much of the news media seems obsessed with reporting problems—almost to the extent of ignoring or excluding solutions."

Jack Nelson, Washington correspondent for the Los Angeles Times, *in 1972*

23
What Happens to Evidence in Court

From all that's been said up to now, it's clear that *the* job of the detective is to gather evidence—and then to identify it in court and testify about the circumstances of its collection.

Naturally you wonder about that evidence. How good is it? How does the prosecution make use of it to secure an indictment and take the case to trial? What does the defense do about that evidence? What part does the judge play in ruling on its validity? And lastly how does the jury evaluate that evidence in deciding whether the defendant is innocent or guilty?

In this chapter you'll learn how cases are tried in American courts of law and what happens to the evidence that detectives search for.

The concept that governs trials is called the *adversary system*. This system is staunchly upheld by most professionals connected with the law and criticized by a minority who find it unfair.

What is the adversary system? It simply consists of rules of procedure meant to keep the judge from taking sides. He or she must hold back on judgment until all the evidence has been examined and all the arguments have been heard. Neither judge nor jury is supposed to take sides on the proceedings. A fair trial requires that each side of the controversy be thoroughly presented. This is where the advocate, the lawyer for the defense, comes in. The advocate's job is to persuade the jury of the rightness of his or her case. Far from being detached, the advocate is expected to present the case in a way that will be most favorable to his or her client. The system expects the accused to be defended by a skilled lawyer, pledged to protect the rights of the accused and to present proofs and reasoned arguments on behalf of the accused. If the accused cannot afford to pay for a lawyer, the court appoints a lawyer to represent him or her.

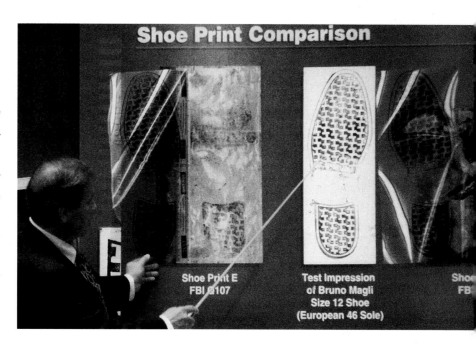

Shoe Print Comparison

Shoe Print E
FBI Q107

Test Impression
of Bruno Magli
Size 12 Shoe
(European 46 Sole)

Sho
FB

Former football star O. J. Simpson underwent a civil trial in 1997 for the murder of his ex-wife and her friend. Evidence of his presence at the crime scene was presented through a comparison of a shoe print left at the crime scene with the Bruno Magli shoes Simpson was known to wear.

It is perfectly proper for a lawyer to take on a criminal case and defend a person whom he or she believes to be guilty. The ethical standards of the legal profession endorse that. The lawyer is not obliged to defend a guilty person. It's up to the lawyer to decide whether he or she wishes to defend a person, no matter how guilty or innocent the accused appears to be. Even lawyers who firmly believe a client is guilty may find some unexpected turn in the evidence that proves the client is innocent. At any rate, what is important under the system is that those accused be defended by lawyers pledged to see that their rights are protected. Lawyers, so the argument goes, are not present in court merely to represent their clients. They also represent society's vital interest in the fundamental process of social decision. Of course, by the rules lawyers are not supposed to cast suspicion on innocent persons in order to free their clients.

The other half of the adversary system is the prosecutor, who also does his or her best to present proofs and arguments to convince the jury that the accused is guilty of whatever crime he or she was brought to trial for.

The adversary procedure is like combat. Its focus is on determining guilt or innocence. It is a battle between opposing lawyers in which "winning" the case becomes the major goal. Technical rules control the admission of evidence, just as the rules for football or basketball guide how the game is played.

What is the thinking behind this adversary system? One law professor has said:

The underlying hope is that if the law permits the lawyer-gladiators to make the fight, out of the clash and clang of their legal or factual battling the rights of the case will appear and justice be done.

But does it work that way? Legal scholars point out that the adversary system sounds good in theory. But to make it operate perfectly, both parties should have the money to pay for thorough investigations. They would need the same good or bad luck in finding witnesses and securing evidence. They should have equal skill in presenting the evidence and organizing their case. Yet it rarely happens that the two sides are roughly equal in these things.

Cleary the adversary method assumes that both sides will be equally matched in means, material, and skill. But that is seldom the case. What happens is that the victory often goes to the powerful rather than to the party who is in the right.

Is that justice? The system's critics do not believe it is. Whom does the system benefit? Usually the rich and the powerful, say the critics. They can buy the expert counsel necessary to win.

Under the adversary system, each side is not obliged to present all it knows, but only its own "best case." Information is avoided or suppressed as eagerly as it is sought. Priority is given to selective representation and misrepresentation in such a win-or-lose trial procedure.

Because the adversary system is by definition either-or, no third person may enter the contest without being placed, by himself or herself or by the court, "for" one side or the other. There is no room for an impartial witness at the trial court (except at the appellate, or appeals, level, where most cases never arrive). So an expert witness is not called for an objective view, for disinterested testimony wherever it may lead; an expert witness is called by a side or for a side. The expert witness is interviewed in advance and chosen only if the testimony will support the side that calls him or her or provide ammunition against the other side. Can such experts be regarded as anything other than partisans? Yet juries are expected to decide which has most convincingly called the other a liar. Couldn't the truth lie somewhere in between or be something that neither side has testified to? Not with a win-or-lose system, say its critics.

One of the essential aspects of the adversary system is the process of cross-examination. After direct examination by their own lawyer has taken place, the opposing lawyers question the other side's witnesses, and they attempt to uncover material hidden or underdeveloped. The witnesses' motives, prejudices, knowledge, and power of memory and description are analyzed by this means. During cross-examination the lawyer tries to obtain helpful testimony and to discredit harmful testimony. The lawyer wants to demean the harmful witness, to cast doubt on his or her truthfulness, to lay the basis for objecting to his or her "incompetent" testimony.

Can truth be the goal for such cross-examination? It is victory the lawyers are after. Manuals of instruction make that clear. Such books, to quote one of them, "advise the lawyer that he has the duty to give the jury, if possible, a false impression of testimony unfavorable to his side."

When a witness is apparently honest, and his or her evidence damaging, the lawyers may twist the cross-examination to suggest that the entire testimony has no importance. One professor of law has put it bluntly:

> It is "ethical" for defense counsel to cross-examine a prosecution witness to make him appear to be inaccurate or untruthful, even when the defense attorney knows that the witness is testifying accurately or truthfully.

Supreme Court Justice Byron White held that if defense counsel can "confuse a witness, even a truthful one, or make him appear at a disadvantage, unsure or indecisive, that will be his normal course." Thus the witness stand has come to be known as "the slaughterhouse of reputations."

Character assassination is a weapon used not only by the defense. The record shows it is employed just as commonly by plaintiffs in civil suits and by the prosecution in criminal cases—or wherever cross-examination comes into play and the goal is winner take all.

A lawyer presents evidence to a judge in court.

24 When the Innocent Are Convicted

What happens when the system of justice goes wrong?

Wrong? Yes—when a person is convicted of a crime, sent to prison, and then found to be innocent.

It happens even in the most extreme case. That is, when someone is convicted of a capital crime, sentenced to death, and then—a "then" that could occur many, many years later—exonerated, or declared to have been not guilty.

Polls indicate that most Americans believe the death penalty is the right punishment for the most atrocious murders. But that faith is based on the assumption that the right person is the one being executed.

Yet a nationwide study shows that in a period of twenty-five years, up to 1998, seventy-four men were exonerated and freed from death row.

Or put it another way: for every 7 executions (486 since 1976), one other prisoner on death row had been found innocent.

That data is so stunning that Gerald Kogen, formerly chief justice of the Florida Supreme Court, said, "If one innocent person is executed along the way, then we can no longer justify capital punishment."

In 2000, as this book was being completed, more than 3,500 inmates awaited execution in the thirty-eight capital punishment states. How many of them are innocent? In one state alone, Illinois, almost as many men (nine) on death row were exonerated as it had executed (eleven).

You may say, don't these facts show that the legal system eventually corrects its mistakes? Not usually. For only one of the nine men released in Illinois got out through the normal appeals process. Most had people outside the system to thank for their freedom. In Illinois, for example, it was a Northwestern

University journalism professor, David Protess, who with four of his students followed leads missed by police and defense attorneys, to tie four other men to the rape and murders that had put four innocent people in prison—for sixteen years before their release.

Studies show that there are several reasons why wrongful convictions happen. One is false confession. People with mild mental retardation often try to conceal their limitations by guessing "right" answers to police questions. Children are especially vulnerable to suggestions by the police. They try to please adults, a danger when police are unscrupulous.

Wrongful capital convictions frequently involve perjured testimony from jailhouse snitches. They claim to have heard a defendant's prison confession, in the hope that it will ease their own punishment. One study found that one of every seven cases involves faulty eyewitness identifications. Those falsely convicted are often outsiders—from a minority group, strangers, passersby.

But the experts agree that the prime reason people are falsely convicted is weak legal representation. A poor person, without the funds to hire his or her own legal counsel, must rely on a court-appointed lawyer. The low fees set by the state cut the suspect off from the best defense. The more experienced lawyers usually set higher fees. And where is the money for the defense to hire skilled investigators to check the evidence presented by detectives or to hire forensic experts to contest those the state can easily afford? In the 1990s sixty-five wrongfully convicted people won release—ten of them from death row—because of DNA testing.

David Protess, journalism professor at Northwestern University, with students who have helped to free prisoners from death row

With his students' help, Professor Barry Scheck of New York's Cardozo Law School has secured the freedom of many wrongfully convicted people by use of DNA evidence.

Professors Barry Scheck and Peter Neufeld, who with their students from the Innocence Project at New York's Cardozo School of Law, helped free thirty-five of those. Their work was considerably hampered because the police often discard evidence used at trial. In 70 percent of the cases these law students investigated, they found that police had discarded semen, hair, or other evidence needed for DNA and other testing.

Even when evidence for DNA tests has not been discarded, it is often not examined. A recent survey ordered by the National Commission for the Future of DNA Evidence found that about 180,000 rape kits sat unexamined in police departments across the nation. There are some 16,000 in New York City alone. The police in some places still test DNA samples only when a suspect has already been arrested. That approach fails to take full advantage of DNA's usefulness for solving crimes.

As DNA data banks expand, it becomes possible to match that evidence, collected in rape, robbery, or other cases, against DNA profiles of convicted offenders or of suspects in other open cases. But that requires more resources to select and test DNA samples.

Science has revolutionized the investigation and prosecution of such cases, but the law hasn't entirely caught up with it. The people at the Innocence Project believe that "criminal investigations can become echo chambers, where answers are shaped by what people believe ought to be true, rather than what they know to be the facts." They suggest that criminal investigations someday soon will begin not with witnesses glancing through books of mug shots but with tissue samples from a crime scene being checked against a database.

It's a great time to rejoice when the wrongfully convicted are freed. But then comes the moment of realization: the guilty persons are still out there, perhaps committing more crimes.

25

So You Want to Be a Detective?

Why would anyone want to join a police force?

It's a hard business, often without letup. Michael Middleton, who spent twenty-one years with the Los Angeles Police Department, said, "It's too grim, often unrelenting." You deal daily with broken human beings. "Sometimes it seems that you never get out of the gutter and you're rolling in garbage day after day."

Yet, he adds, there's another side of police work that's positive. "It's about all the good people and the good things they do. It's about remembering that you have negative contacts with only a small part of society. If you remember and focus only on the bad parts of the job, it will consume you, and you'll never appreciate all the positive things you see and the good you can do. You have to be able to keep a balance."

Thomas McKenna said he became a detective because "it offered respect in your profession, job security, good benefits, and a structured work environment."

Men and women who aspire to be detectives don't leap into that job as soon as they join a police force. To be a detective they must first gain experience as a uniformed police officer. After several years in that duty, an officer may be promoted to detective. "May," because there is nothing certain about it. How the promotion happens varies from department to department or from commanding officer to commanding officer. In some departments the hopefuls have to pass both written and oral examinations and then enter a training program lasting from a few weeks to several months. In New York City, police academy training for a detective is six months, followed by six months of field training before assignment to a precinct.

Students in a classroom discussion at the John Jay College of Criminal Justice in New York City

Once having reached that level, detectives no longer wear the police uniform but go about in street clothing—"plainclothes," they call it. The new detective is assigned as a trainee to a veteran on the force. They become partners, with the rookie learning on the job from the oldtimer. In a city with a big police force, detectives work in specialized units, such as narcotics, arson, homicide, gambling, or robbery.

Work is done both at a department desk and out in the field. An investigation starts when a police officer (or a civilian) calls in to report a crime. Then detectives move out to the scene to look for the answers to those six questions: Who? What? When? Where? How? Why?

If you're interested in detective work as a career, it's helpful to take a variety of courses in high school and college: English, American history, government, sociology, psychology, chemistry, biology. And with America's population becoming more and more diverse, a foreign language would be an asset. Essential too are skills in typing and the use of computers.

Your job chances are improved if you go on to college and earn a bachelor's or graduate degree. Police departments sometimes require college degrees of applicants.

Students interested in work as criminologists should study those specialized fields in which they'd like to work: chemistry, biology, electronics, or whatever field is appropriate. Some colleges offer courses in the forensic sciences.

Are you the right type? Is there such a thing as a "police type"? They say no. All kinds of people come and go. You don't change who you are just because you swear an oath to uphold the law and carry a gun. That doesn't make a hero out of you. No one is fearless doing this kind of work. McKenna sums up what the life is like:

> The average officer works eight hours a day. Seven hours and fifty-nine minutes he spends serving the community one way or another. Sometimes in that one other minute he looks fear in the face. If he does his job in spite of fear, that makes the guy with the badge different and special. That one minute binds him and his partner in a brotherhood that forms when two men meet danger and survive. The adventure of the job is that you never know when danger will come or how often. It's just a reality you have to deal with.

Graduation day for cadets at the Los Angeles Police Department police academy

Bibliography

The impulse for this book came when I was reading a true story about a terrible murder in the early 1900s and the long trial that followed. *Big Trouble,* by J. Anthony Lukas, deals in rich detail with the assistance given the prosecution by a star detective of the famous Pinkerton Agency.

I knew a little about the art of detection from reading mystery novels and from both true and fictional stories of crime in the press, the movies, and on radio and TV. But Lukas's history made me want to learn a lot more. (That's often how books are born—out of curiosity.)

The principal sources for this book are listed alphabetically.

Anderson, David, and Peter Benjaminson. *Investigative Reporting.* Bloomington: Indiana University Press, 1976.

Benjaminson, Peter. *Secret Police: Inside the New York City Department of Correction.* New York: Barricade, 1997.

Bergman, Paul. *The Criminal Law Handbook.* Berkeley: Nolo, 1997.

Bonovolonte, Jules, and Brian Duffy. *The Good Guys.* New York: Simon & Schuster, 1996.

Buchanan, Edna. *The Corpse Had a Familiar Face.* New York: Random House, 1987.

———. *Never Let Them See You Cry.* New York: Random House, 1992.

Cohen, Paul, and Shari Cohen. *Careers in Law Enforcement and Security.* New York: Rosen, 1995.

Corwin, Miles. *The Killing Season.* New York: Simon & Schuster, 1997.

Count, E. W. *Cop Talk: True Detective Stories from the New York Police Department.* New York: Pocket Books, 1994.

Cummings, Richard. *Be Your Own Detective.* New York: McKay, 1980.

Davidson, James West, and Mark A. Lytle. *After the Fact: The Art of Historical Detection.* New York: McGraw-Hill, 1999.

DeForest, Peter R., R. E. Gaenssten, and Henry C. Lee. *Forensic Science: An Introduction to Criminalistics.* New York: McGraw-Hill, 1983.

Ettema, James S., and Theodore L. Glasser. *Custodians of Conscience: Investigative Journalism and Public Virtue.* New York: Columbia, 1998.

Evans, Colin. *The Casebook of Forensic Detection.* New York: Viking, 1996.

Friedman, Lawrence M. *Crime and Punishment in American History.* New York: Basic Books, 1993.

———. *A History of American Law.* New York: Simon & Schuster, 1985.

Humes, Edward. *Mean Justice: A Town's Terror, a Prosecutor's Power, and a Betrayal of Innocence.* New York: Simon & Schuster, 1999.

Jones, Richard Glynn, ed. *Poison! The World's Greatest True Murder Stories.* Secaucus, N.J.: Lyle Stuart, 1987.

Kaminer, Wendy. *It's All the Rage: Crime and Culture.* New York: Addison-Wesley, 1995.

Kelly, John F., and Philip K. Wearne. *Tainting Evidence: Inside the Scandals at the FBI Crime Lab.* New York: Free Press, 1998.

Klaidman, Stephen, and Tom L. Beauchamp. *The Virtuous Journalist.* New York: Oxford, 1987.

Lardner, James. *Crusader: The Hell-Raising Police Career of Detective David Durk.* New York: Random House,1996.

Loftus, Elizabeth F. *Eyewitness Testimony.* Cambridge, Mass.: Harvard University Press, 1996.

Loftus, Elizabeth F., and Katherine Ketchams. *Witness for the Defense.* New York: St. Martin's Press, 1991.

Lukas, J. Anthony. *Big Trouble.* New York: Simon & Schuster, 1997.

Mackay, James. *Allan Pinkerton: The First Private Eye.* New York: Wiley, 1996.

McKenna, Thomas, and William Harrington. *Manhattan North Homicide.* New York: St. Martin's Press, 1996.

Meltzer, Milton. *Crime in America.* New York: Morrow, 1990.

Middleton, Michael. *Cop: A True Story.* Chicago: Contemporary, 1994.

Millimaki, Robert H. *Fingerprint Detection.* Philadelphia: Lippincott, 1961.

————. *The Making of a Detective.* Philadelphia: Lippincott, 1976.

Morn, Frank. *"The Eye That Never Sleeps": A History of the Pinkerton National Detective Agency.* Bloomington: Indiana University Press, 1982.

National Institute of Law Enforcement and Criminal Justice. *The Criminal Investigative Process: A Dialogue on Research Findings.* Washington, D.C.: U.S. Department of Justice, April 1997.

Nickell, Joe, and John F. Fischer. *Crime Science: Methods of Forensic Detection.* Lexington: University of Kentucky Press, 1998.

Nolan, William. Hammett: *A Life at the Edge.* New York: Congdon and Weed, 1983.

Pepinsky, Harold E., and Paul Jesilow. *Myths That Cause Crime.* Cabin John, Md.: Seven Locks, 1984.

Pinkerton, Allan. *Criminal Reminiscences and Detective Sketches.* New York: Garrett, 1969.

Pistone, Joseph, with Richard Woodley. *Donnie Brasco: My Undercover Life in the Mafia.* New York: New American, 1988.

Protess, David, and Robert Warden. *A Promise of Justice.* New York: Hyperion, 1998.

Pulitzer, Lisa Beth. *Crime on Deadline.* New York: Boulevard, 1996.

Revell, Oliver "Buck," and Dwight Williams. *A G-Man's Journal.* New York: Pocket Books, 1998.

Saferstein, Richard. *Criminalistics: An Introduction to Forensic Science,* 6th ed. New York: Prentice Hall, 1998.

Scheck, Barry, et al. *Actual Innocence: Five Days to Execution, and Other Dispatches from the Wrongfully Convicted.* New York: Doubleday, 2000.

Shapiro, Fred R., and Jane Garry. *Trial and Error: An Oxford Anthology of Legal Stories.* New York: Oxford, 1998.

Strick, Anne. *Injustice Is All.* New York: Penguin, 1978.

Theoharis, Athan G., ed. *The FBI: A Comprehensive Reference Guide.* New York: Oryx, 1998.

Vila, Bryan, and Cynthia Morris, eds. *The Role of Police in American Society.* Westport, Ct.: Greenwood, 1999.

Volkman, Ernest. *Gangbusters: The Destruction of America's Last Mafia Dynasty.* New York: Faber, 1998.

Weinberg, Steve. *The Reporter's Handbook: An Investigative Guide to Documents and Techniques,* 3rd ed. New York: St. Martin's Press, 1996.

Whitaker, Reg. *The End of Privacy: How Total Surveillance Is Becoming a Reality.* New York: New Press, 1999.

Wormser, Richard. *Pinkerton.* New York: Walker & Co., 1990.

I also made extensive use of the files of the *New York Times.*

Photo Credits

Page 1, Versace murder scene: © De Keerle/FSP/Gamma
Page 4, Jonathan Wild: © Hulton Getty Archive/Liaison
Page 5, saloon arrest: © Hulton Getty Archive/Liaison
Page 7, Holmes and Watson: © Hulton Getty Archive/Liaison
Page 8, lab researcher: AP/Ed Andrieski
Page 10, Sir Alexander Fleming: AP
Page 10, penicillin in a petri dish: AP/Wide World Photos
Page 12, Lindbergh ladder: © Bettmann/CORBIS
Page 12, Lindbergh baby picture: AP
Page 13, bloodstained wood: AP Photo/Mark Duncan
Page 15, detective talking to witness: © Steve Liss/Gamma Liaison Network
Page 16, officer talking to boy: Steve Liss/Liaison
Page 17, Gerry Adams with a bugging device: Paul McErlane/Archive
Page 22, cocaine bust: Anthony Bolante/Archive
Page 25, lab technician: Chester Higgins, Jr./NYT Pictures
Page 29, bags of forensic evidence: Cory Sipkin/Gamma Liaison
Page 31, fingerprint microchip: AP Wide World Photos
Page 34, bar-coding DNA: © Richard T. Nowitz/CORBIS
Page 37, bullets and firearms test: Jose Nicholas/Saola, Getty Liaison
Page 42, Hanna and Laszlo Sulner: AP/Wide World Photos
Page 43, Hauptmann kidnap note: © Bettmann/CORBIS
Page 44, Konrad Kujau: AP
Page 46, lie detection test: © Richard T. Nowitz/CORBIS
Page 49, forensic exam of skull: © Francis Demange/Getty Liaison
Page 50, daguerreotype of Lincoln: AP
Page 52, skeletons of czar and family: AP
Page 53, scientists with 1,000-year-old mummy: AP
Page 55, Allan Pinkerton: CORBIS
Page 59, Pinkerton and Lincoln: © Hulton Getty Archive
Page 61, Homestead Strike engraving: © Bettmann/CORBIS
Page 63, Spy World store: Tobias Everke/Getty Liaison
Page 66, "Lucky" Luciano: AP/Wide World Photos
Page 68, Gambino crime family: AP/Wide World Photos
Page 71, Betty Tyson: Wayne Scarsberry/Liaison
Page 73, Jack Nelson: AP/Wide World Photos
Page 75, O. J. Simpson evidence: John Barr/Gamma Liaison
Page 77, lawyer presenting evidence: CORBIS
Page 79, David Protess and students: Maggie Steber/SABA
Page 80, Barry Scheck: AP
Page 82, John Jay College classroom scene: John Jay College Public Relations Department
Page 83, police academy graduation: Roger Sandler/Gamma Liaison